SURPR

Frank and Joe weaved their way through the maze of trailers on the movie set until they found the one marked F/X, for special effects. Frank still didn't like the idea of donning makeup to play a zombie in a horror movie, but Joe could hardly wait.

"Wait till you meet Paula West," Joe said, starting up the steps to her trailer. "Not only is she one of the best in this business, she's gorgeous besides."

"Oh, then I guess she can't be a suspect, right?" Frank kidded. "Let's get ready to join the dead. Or is it the undead?"

As Joe reached for the trailer door, Frank noticed that it had opened slightly. To his surprise, an arm emerged.

It was clutching a knife!

"Watch out." Frank lunged forward to knock Joe out of the way.

Too late. As Frank shouted in fear, the knife plunged toward Joe's chest!

Books in THE HARDY BOYS CASEFILES™ Series

#1 DEAD ON TARGET
#2 EVIL, INC.
#3 CULT OF CRIME
#4 THE LAZARUS PLOT
#5 EDGE OF DESTRUCTION
#6 THE CROWNING TERROR
#7 DEATHGAME
#8 SEE NO EVIL
#9 THE GENIUS THIEVES
#10 HOSTAGES OF HATE
#11 BROTHER AGAINST BROTHER
#12 PERFECT GETAWAY
#13 THE BORGIA DAGGER
#14 TOO MANY TRAITORS
#15 BLOOD RELATIONS
#16 LINE OF FIRE
#17 THE NUMBER FILE
#18 A KILLING IN THE MARKET
#19 NIGHTMARE IN ANGEL CITY
#20 WITNESS TO MURDER
#21 STREET SPIES
#22 DOUBLE EXPOSURE
#23 DISASTER FOR HIRE
#24 SCENE OF THE CRIME
#25 THE BORDERLINE CASE
#26 TROUBLE IN THE PIPELINE
#27 NOWHERE TO RUN
#28 COUNTDOWN TO TERROR
#29 THICK AS THIEVES
#30 THE DEADLIEST DARE
#31 WITHOUT A TRACE
#32 BLOOD MONEY
#33 COLLISION COURSE
#34 FINAL CUT
#35 THE DEAD SEASON
#36 RUNNING ON EMPTY
#37 DANGER ZONE
#38 DIPLOMATIC DECEIT
#39 FLESH AND BLOOD
#40 FRIGHT WAVE
#41 HIGHWAY ROBBERY
#42 THE LAST LAUGH
#43 STRATEGIC MOVES
#44 CASTLE FEAR
#45 IN SELF-DEFENSE
#46 FOUL PLAY
#47 FLIGHT INTO DANGER
#48 ROCK 'N' REVENGE
#49 DIRTY DEEDS
#50 POWER PLAY
#51 CHOKE HOLD
#52 UNCIVIL WAR
#53 WEB OF HORROR

Available from ARCHWAY Paperbacks

THE HAR
BOY
CASE

WEB OF

FRANKLI

AN ARCHWAY PAPERBACK
Published by POCKET BOOKS
New York London Toronto Sydney Tokyo Singapore

AN ARCHWAY PAPERBACK *Original*

An Archway Paperback published by
POCKET BOOKS, a division of Simon & Schuster Inc.
1230 Avenue of the Americas, New York, NY 10020

ISBN: 0-671-73089-4

First Archway Paperback printing July 1991

10 9 8 7 6 5 4 3 2 1

Cover art by Brian Kotzky

Printed in the U.S.A.

IL 6+

WEB OF HORROR

Chapter 1

"HELP ME!" Joe Hardy heard the man scream. Joe sat up taller in his chair and tried to peer through the thick mist that filled the room, but he couldn't even see his older brother, Frank, who was sitting right next to him.

"Please, someone help me!" the voice pleaded again, hoarse with fear.

Gradually the mist began to disperse, and Joe was able to make out a young man wearing a high school letter jacket and designer jeans sitting on a sofa. His terror-filled eyes were focused on a point beyond the Hardys.

As Joe watched, the high school student was seized by two scaly arms that seemed to grow out of the sofa. The young man screamed and tried to squirm away, but it was no use.

The monstrous arms slowly pulled the student down, and unbelievably he disappeared between the cushions of the sofa!

"Cut!" a loud voice shouted.

With the flick of a light switch the scene of supernatural horror was instantly transformed to that of a movie set.

Joe put his hands up to his blue eyes to shield them from the bright light that now filled the room.

Joe took a deep breath and stood up to stretch his six-foot frame. He watched as two crew members shoved the sofa aside, revealing a trapdoor beneath it. The door opened, and out crawled the actor who had just been devoured by the monster couch.

Joe poked Frank in the ribs. "Oh, man, wasn't that great?"

Frank just sighed and tried to smile as he ran his fingers back through his dark hair.

Joe couldn't believe what a drag his brother was being. "I don't get it. I was sure you'd be psyched to help Dad with security on the set of this movie. I mean—" Joe's attention was caught by a redheaded, fair-skinned woman in her early twenties, who was removing the arms from the sofa. She must be on the special-effects crew, Joe thought, and watched her pick up the arms and a remote-control device and head toward them.

"If you keep sulking, you won't make a good

impression on the beauty heading our way," Joe muttered to Frank.

Frank glanced at the young woman, but he didn't seem to be interested.

Joe flashed the woman the broadest smile he could muster as she passed by. His smile curved down as the redhead continued on her way, oblivious of either Joe or Frank.

"You barely glanced at her," Joe said to Frank.

"She was okay. But there would be lots more girls to look at on the beach. That's where most people go on their summer vacations. Somewhere with surfboards and the ocean. What are we doing in the middle of Texas? All we get to see here are cows, tumbleweed, and dust."

Joe frowned. Frank's attitude was ruining the fun he planned to have helping his father with the security on the movie set of *Horror House Five: Back from the Grave,* which was being shot on location in Beaufort, Texas. The *Horror House* series was loosely based on a documented haunting incident, and the films were made at the house where the haunting supposedly occurred.

Fenton Hardy, a former New York City police detective turned private investigator, had been hired by his friend Leonard Gold, the head of Fourteen Karat Studios, the New York-based company that produced the *Horror House* series, to head their security team. Die-hard fans eager to steal props or worm their way into a scene had always made top security a necessity for the production company.

"Come on, Frank," said Joe. "Don't you think it's cool to see what goes on behind the scenes?"

Joe motioned toward the living room. The crew was disassembling equipment to move it upstairs, where the next scene would be shot. Already the living room was resembling its former state. Like the other rooms in the house, it was rustic but well kept. The floors were hardwood, and the walls were wood paneled. The flagstone fireplace was huge. The house was over eighty years old, and with the right lighting it was the most ominous-looking place Joe had ever seen. He could understand why the production company wanted to film at the house.

"You don't think this is interesting?" Joe asked.

"Sure," Frank said, "if you're into this kind of stuff. But we've been on movie sets before. I'm just not all that crazy about slasher flicks."

Before Joe could reply, he was interrupted by the director, Shane Katz, making an announcement.

"Put that last cut in the can and let's hope there was enough mist to make those reptilian arms look real."

Joe smiled to himself. He knew enough movie lingo to understand that the last take of the monster sofa scene would be developed and printed for Katz to view later in a private screening room at Fourteen Karat Studios in Dallas. Each scene was also videotaped on a camcorder. That way the director could get an immediate idea of what had been filmed. But Joe knew there was really no way to be sure a scene was going to work until it was previewed on a big screen.

Joe watched as Katz rubbed the back of his neck. The director wore faded jeans and a T-shirt. With his dark, graying hair and full beard, he seemed about forty. His eyes were bloodshot, and the dark circles under them didn't surprise Joe. He knew the long and grueling hours the director put in.

"What's the problem, people?"

Joe turned as the speaker came charging out of the kitchen and into the living room. He had shoulder-length blond hair and a round, childlike head set on a fairly thin body. Joe recognized him from interviews as Andrew Warmouth, the film's producer. As Warmouth wormed his way into the middle of the living room next to Katz, he glared at the crew. They instantly sped up the moving process.

"Why are we behind schedule?" Warmouth bellowed. "We're making a cheap horror movie, not *Gone With the Wind*. The couch scene should have been in the can already! Let's get this train back on the track, people!"

"You heard the man," Katz said through cupped hands. "Let's move it."

Warmouth nodded to Katz, then turned and barreled out of the room.

"What a sweetheart," Frank mumbled.

"Producers have to be that way, Frank," Joe said. "There are only four to six weeks to get this film shot. Nothing would get done if Warmouth wasn't breathing down everyone's neck constantly."

Joe felt a heavy hand on his shoulder and turned to find his father standing behind him.

"Enjoying yourselves, boys?" Fenton asked.

"One of us is," Joe said.

"Give me a break, Joe. I told you—I just don't like horror movies," Frank protested.

"Can't blame you for that," Fenton said, smiling. "I don't care for the blood-and-guts stuff myself."

"Where's your sense of humor, guys?" Joe said.

Joe listened as Shane Katz boomed out, "Dinner break, everyone. It's six o'clock. Be back in one hour, and we'll set up for the 'bathtub of blood' scene."

Joe laughed as the actor who had been sucked into the sofa groaned at the news.

"You boys had better go grab a bite," Fenton said. "The production company has a catering service lined up for tomorrow, but tonight we have to fend for ourselves. Would you mind bringing me back a tuna melt and a coffee? I have some work to do in my trailer."

"Sure," Frank said.

As Joe was about to leave, he spotted a small, timid-looking man standing beside the front door of the house. He was in his late thirties, stood about five-seven, and weighed about one hundred fifty pounds, Joe estimated. The man was balding, with thick bifocals, and he had a nervous tic that made the right side of his face jump. He wore a gray, ill-fitting suit and was carrying a *Horror House* script.

"Oh, my gosh, Frank!" Joe whispered excitedly. "It's him! It's the Reaper!"

Joe couldn't believe he was standing so close to Matthew Clervi, the man who played the Reaper, the supernatural creature who always lurked inside the Horror House. His character had become so famous that Reaper T-shirts were selling out in stores all over the country.

"Where?" Frank asked, looking past the little man.

Joe realized that Frank was expecting a hooded, red-eyed, skeletal beast. "Right there," Joe said softly, pointing. "The guy in the bifocals and gray suit."

"You've got to be kidding." Frank laughed. "He's the guy who runs around in a hood and robe, hacking up people with a scythe?"

"Yes," Joe insisted. "That's Matthew Clervi. He's the star."

Clervi made it out of the house just then, having more than a little trouble opening the heavy front door.

"He looks more like a librarian than a slasher or actor," Frank said.

"He used to be a serious actor. Before he became the Reaper, he did a lot of Shakespeare."

"And he broadened his career with this role," Frank said sarcastically. "What a dramatic challenge, hiding in shadows and jumping out at innocent people."

"His best role to date," Joe said. He lurked behind Frank, imitating the Reaper.

"Come on, killer," Frank said. "Let's go hack up a cheeseburger."

Joe pressed his cold glass of lemonade against his forehead and sighed with relief. The temperature in Beaufort was ninety-five degrees even at six o'clock, and the only respite from the heat the Mid-Way Café offered, besides something cool to drink, was an ancient ceiling fan that barely stirred the heavy air. Sprawled out in a corner booth, Joe waited for Frank to finish his supper.

"What I don't understand is how these kinds of movies can claim to be based on actual events," Frank said, finishing off his chocolate shake.

"*Horror House* is," Joe said.

Frank laughed. "Come on."

"You mean you've never heard the story of the Hughes house?"

Frank hesitated.

"The very house that *Horror House Five* is being filmed in is said to be haunted. You know—there were reports of strange noises, moving objects, cold rooms . . . the whole bit. The people who lived there, Harold and Kitty Hughes, wrote a book about what they experienced. Shane Katz was a beginning director at the time, and he said the book inspired him to make a movie about it. He finally got mega-producer Andrew Warmouth to back him. The movies have all been filmed here at the actual house."

"People honestly think the house is haunted?" Frank asked skeptically.

"Actually, there hasn't been an incident in ten years," Joe said.

"Maybe there weren't any incidents to begin with."

"You're so closed-minded," Joe said with an exasperated grin.

"So what about this Reaper character?" Frank asked. "Where did he come from?"

"The Reaper is Katz's creation. He was added to the series for suspense, not to mention marketing potential. Haunted houses are just backdrops nowadays."

Frank nodded and picked up the bill. "Let's get back to the set with Dad's food."

"Let's do him a favor and forget his dinner," Joe groaned, rubbing his stomach.

"What's the matter?" Frank said, grinning. "Doesn't the Mid-Way Café agree with you?"

"Yeah, the Mid-Way Café," Joe muttered. "Midway between heartburn and food poisoning."

"What did you think of the bathtub of blood scene?" Joe asked Frank as they walked toward their trailer later that night. It was after eleven and the Hardys were finally heading for bed.

"It was gross," Frank said.

"Well," Joe said, "I thought it was cool. That fake blood sure looked real, didn't it? I guess they'll use a lot of it tomorrow. Katz said they're doing a scene with the Reaper."

"I can hardly wait," Frank muttered.

Joe wearily climbed the single step of their small trailer, which had barely enough room to turn around in when the two beds were pulled down.

"Why did Dad leave the set early?" Frank asked as he and Joe got ready for bed.

"I think he went out to buy antacid," Joe said.

Frank laughed. "We warned him."

Joe turned off the lamp on the nightstand between the beds.

"Good night, Joe," Frank said, turning on his side.

"Good night, and don't let the Reaper bite." Joe laughed maniacally as he shut the light off.

Just as the boys fell asleep they were awakened by a woman screaming. Joe and Frank leapt from their beds, threw on their jeans, and charged toward the noise of an excited crowd. At the house the film crew was gathered at the front door. Joe and Frank pushed partway through the crowd, but eventually got bogged down near the entrance. The crew had completely blocked their way.

"We're with security!" Joe shouted in frustration. "Let us through!"

Finally Joe made it to the door. He thrust out his arm to keep Frank from stumbling into their father, who was blocking the doorway.

"What happened, Dad?" Joe asked, feeling the crowd press against his back.

"They just found Andrew Warmouth's body," Fenton said gravely. "He was killed tonight—cut down with the Reaper's scythe!"

Chapter 2

JOE STARED at Warmouth's lifeless body where it lay three or four feet inside the house. The producer had collapsed forward onto the floor. At the back of his neck was an ugly wound. Blood had soaked through most of his shirt and the floor under him.

Joe ran upstairs and found a sheet in a linen closet to lay over Warmouth's body. When he came back down, he saw that three more of his father's security guards had arrived to keep the crowd back until the police could show up.

Joe poked his head into the den. His dad was questioning the redheaded young woman Joe had spotted during the monster couch scene. Joe went back and joined Frank, who was staring down at the covered corpse.

"What do you make of it?" Frank asked.

"He was obviously struck from behind. Our trailer is close enough to the house to hear Warmouth scream if he'd known what was coming," Joe said. "The killer must have gotten to him before he had a chance to turn around. He probably never knew what hit him."

"That wound on the back of his neck is huge," Frank said. "The only thing that could have left a mark that size is a scythe."

"The trademark weapon of the Reaper," Joe said. "That's what Dad said, too."

"That woman he's talking to is the one who screamed," Frank told his brother. "Her name's Cathleen Bowley. She's the makeup special-effects assistant. Let's go see what Dad's found out."

As Frank and Joe started toward the den, Joe noticed a rotund man in a sheriff's uniform entering the house. With him were Shane Katz and a young deputy.

"Who are you boys?" the sheriff asked, checking out the Hardys.

"I'm Joe Hardy, and this is my brother, Frank. We've just arrived, and we're with security," Joe said.

"Security?" the sheriff scoffed. "I thought we had child labor laws in Texas."

Joe opened his mouth to answer, but just then his father joined them.

"I'm Fenton Hardy," the detective said to the

sheriff. "I'm head of security. These are my sons, Joe and Frank."

"Rhett Thornall, sheriff of Beaufort." The sheriff shook Fenton's hand. "What have we got here?"

"Take a look for yourself," Joe said, still fuming over Thornall's earlier sarcastic remark.

Thornall gently lifted the sheet from Warmouth's body. "That's nasty," Thornall muttered. He raised his eyes to Fenton. "Who was he?"

"Andrew Warmouth. The film's producer."

"Any witnesses?" Thornall asked.

"Just a young lady who found the body," Fenton replied. "She's still in shock."

Katz, who had peered over Thornall's shoulder, was muttering and shaking his head in disbelief. "Poor Andy," he repeated over and over.

"Well, you fellas can clear out now," Thornall said to the Hardys. "I'll take it from here. My deputy will round up the crew for questioning."

"Wait a minute. You can't march in here and tell us to get lost," Joe said. "We work here!"

Thornall chuckled. "Now, look, I have a forensics team heading down from Dallas, and they sure don't need a bunch of rent-a-cops getting in their way. If you want to be useful, why don't you take Mr. Katz back to his trailer? He looks pretty shook up."

Joe opened his mouth to say something else, but Fenton took him by the arm and steered him out of the house. Frank followed with Shane Katz.

"I'll be okay," Katz insisted, though he still looked as if he was on the verge of collapse. "I talked to Leonard Gold before the sheriff arrived. He wants us to meet at his Dallas office tomorrow morning."

"Then we'd all better get some sleep," Fenton suggested.

Even Frank was impressed by Leonard Gold's Dallas office. A huge penthouse on the top floor of a downtown business complex, it was one of the most plush layouts he had ever seen. "And this is just a branch office," he reminded himself. The success of the *Horror House* series had allowed Fourteen Karat Studios to expand from its small New York headquarters and set up another office in Dallas.

From his place between Joe and his father at a conference table in the center of the room, Frank could easily watch Sheriff Thornall and Shane Katz across from him and still see Leonard Gold at the head of the table.

Gold stood up and gripped the table. He was a tall, stern-faced man in an expensive white suit. "Thank you for coming, gentlemen," he began, sweeping them briefly with his eyes. "As you know, Andrew Warmouth was brutally murdered last night. The person responsible for this crime must be brought to justice—and fast. Gentlemen, I need your suggestions."

Gold sat back down, pushing his gold-framed glasses up on the bridge of his nose. "Sheriff Thornall," he said, "we'll start with you."

Thornall stood up. "Well, we're pretty sure Warmouth was struck on the back of the neck by the scythe y'all use in your movies," he said. "We had a forensics team out there most of last night searching for a print or strand of hair from the killer, but so many people had been crawling all over that house, it was impossible."

I wish Joe and I could have tried, Frank thought.

"Mmm," Gold grunted, a disturbed expression on his face. "Any suspects?"

"Two, so far," Thornall said. "The young lady who found his body, Cathleen Bowley—"

"Excuse me, Sheriff," interrupted Fenton Hardy, "but isn't Miss Bowley too small to have nearly decapitated someone as tall as Warmouth?"

"Never underestimate a woman, Mr. Hardy," Thornall said.

"Who is the other suspect?" Gold asked.

"Matthew Clervi," Thornall said.

Leonard Gold gasped. "That can't be possible. If Matthew Clervi is guilty, it'll ruin us. We'd have to fold the *Horror House* series because he has too big a following to replace." He frowned. "Besides, Clervi's a teddy bear. Everyone knows he's harmless."

"He knows how to wield the scythe, and he doesn't have an alibi," Thornall said.

"We saw Clervi yesterday before the dinner break," Frank spoke up. "He seemed quite nervous."

"He always looks like that," Gold said.

"I'm sorry if it would hurt your business, Mr. Gold," Thornall said, "but Clervi is a suspect."

"Ridiculous," Gold insisted. "Anything further, Sheriff?"

"Yes, in fact, I'm going to have to ask you to halt production and close that house down before anyone else gets hurt."

"He's right, Leonard." It was Shane Katz, who had remained silent all morning. "Andy's dead! I think we should cut our losses and film the rest of the movie later. Andy was my friend, and I don't know if I'm up to finishing the film right now."

"We can't halt production!" Gold said incredulously. "Don't get me wrong. If it were my money backing this project, I'd take the loss, no problem. But we have several overseas investors who have a lot to lose if this film isn't completed on schedule.

"We all know Andy was very difficult. I'd even bet you're the only person Andy called a friend. My feeling is that whoever killed Warmouth wanted Warmouth only, and I think everyone else on the set is safe."

"Are you saying you're going to buck my

request?" Thornall said. "There's a killer on the loose."

"Sheriff Thornall has a point," Joe spoke up. "It's going to be hard to find evidence with a house full of people."

"That's where you and your brother enter the picture," Gold announced. He turned back to the sheriff. "Sheriff, I know this isn't your only case. You can't always be on the set, searching for clues. And even if you could, it would interfere with the filming. How about a compromise? You let me finish my movie, and I put Joe and Frank Hardy into the film."

"What are you talking about, Leonard?" Katz asked.

"Well, in the *Horror House* movies, the Reaper's victims always return as zombie slaves to serve the Reaper. I want Joe and Frank to go undercover and play zombies in the movie. They've just arrived, so very few people know they're with security."

Frank groaned inwardly. It was bad enough to have to work on the set, but to actually appear in this creature feature? He wondered what his girlfriend, Callie Shaw, would say when she found out. She hated gore films even more than Frank did. Frank glanced at his brother. Joe was beaming at the suggestion.

Sheriff Thornall, though, obviously wasn't happy. "I don't know how things are done up North where you come from," he said, "but in these parts, Mr. Gold, investigations are left to professionals. These two boys are greenhorns. They're barely old enough to shave."

Frank looked at Joe. He could tell his brother was fuming.

"We greenhorns have probably solved more cases than you can count," Joe said sharply.

"Fenton will still be heading the investigation," Gold assured the sheriff. "Don't worry about Frank and Joe, Sheriff. They're far more experienced than their years. As for Fenton, believe me, if I could use him as a zombie, I'd put him undercover, too. But everyone already knows he's head of security."

"Well, Leonard, if there's nothing more, I think we'd better head back to Beaufort," Fenton Hardy said after waiting for another objection from the sheriff.

"I think we've covered everything we can," Gold said. "See what you find out, and keep me posted."

Thornall stood up, hat in hand. "I'll check in with you as often as I can," he said. "If you want, I'll station a man at the Hughes house. It won't be easy to spare anyone right now, though, with everyone pouring into Beaufort. I tell you, son, every time a new *Horror House* movie's made, they just about destroy Beaufort. My neighborhood in particular. I live right down the street from the Hughes house. Anyway, here are my phone numbers, office and home. I expect to be consulted, and we'll update you on our investigation, also."

Thornall handed Fenton a piece of paper.

"I'll do that, Sheriff," Fenton said.

Then Thornall turned to Katz. "I'll be by later to question Clervi again."

"You'd better make it this evening. I think he'll be shooting a scene this afternoon—with the zombies," Katz said, nodding toward the Hardys.

Thornall shook his head and left the room.

"You guys need to be in makeup by two o'clock," Katz informed the Hardys. His expression softened, and he added almost to himself, "I don't like this at all. Andy's body is still warm, and we're forging ahead as if nothing's happened."

Before Katz left, he paused and turned back to the Hardys. "I want you to know I appreciate your efforts. Andy Warmouth was my friend." Frank and Joe watched sympathetically as the director left the office.

"Well," Fenton Hardy said to his sons after the three of them had walked to their rented car, parked in the underground parking lot. "It's a forty-five-minute drive from Dallas to Beaufort. If you guys have a game plan, let's hear it."

"I think Thornall has the wrong suspects," Joe said, getting into the seat in the front. Frank climbed into the back, stretching out with his arms folded behind his head.

"Why do you think that?" asked Frank.

"His evidence is all circumstantial," Joe replied. "Cathy is a suspect because she found Warmouth's body. Clervi is a suspect because a prop he uses in the movie was the murder weapon. If you were Clervi and you wanted to kill someone, would you use the scythe?"

"No," Frank said, "but if I were someone else and I wanted to kill Warmouth, I might use the scythe hoping to incriminate Clervi."

"I say that we examine the murder area again when we get back to the set," Fenton said. "Looks like you'll have to get your hands dirty, you pair of greenhorns."

Frank and Joe and Fenton got back around eleven-thirty and went into the house, checking through it thoroughly. The crew was working in silence with sullen or frightened expressions. Frank shook his head grimly. The saying "The show must go on" had taken on a very dark meaning since the night before.

After an hour or so the Hardys all met back at the front door to study the taped outline of Warmouth's body on the hall floor. "Warmouth must have just walked into the house, taken a few steps, and been struck almost immediately from behind," Fenton said. "But where was the killer?"

"There's only one place the killer could have used." Frank motioned to the small closet beside the front door.

"You're right," Joe said. "If the killer had come in through the front door, Warmouth would have turned around. That door is heavy and makes a lot of noise, and Warmouth had no idea someone was behind him."

Fenton borrowed a penlight from Joe and stepped into the closet. A few moments later he emerged.

"Nothing in there but a jacket that looks about a hundred years old and the biggest collection of mothballs I've ever seen," Fenton said, brushing dust off his sleeves.

"So what's next?" Joe asked.

"We should talk to Cathleen Bowley and Matthew Clervi. I understand Thornall's men also questioned Katz's assistant, Mike Sinnochi, last night. He was around at the time the murder occurred, so we should question him, too," Frank suggested. "Cathy told Dad that she saw Sinnochi outside right before she found Warmouth's body."

Fenton looked at his watch. "It's close to one o'clock. You guys had better head over to the makeup trailer. I'll try questioning some more of the crew. We'll meet later this afternoon."

Frank and Joe headed for the trailer where Paula West, one of the best special-effects makeup wizards in the horror movie industry, would be waiting for them. Frank knew all about her, thanks to Joe.

The old Hughes house didn't appear to be spooky that day—just kind of run-down. Located on an acre of property in a section of Beaufort that had gone to seed, the Victorian mansion was surrounded by trailers in which the crew worked and slept. Frank searched among the trailers until he spotted one with a small plywood sign tacked to it that read F/X.

Frank still didn't like the idea of playing a zombie in a horror movie. His only hope was that the makeup would hide him so completely that his friends wouldn't recognize him. He made a mental note to be sure Katz left his name out of the credits.

"Wait till you meet Paula West," Joe said. "Not only is she one of the best in this business, she's gorgeous besides."

"Oh, then I guess she can't be a suspect, right?" Frank kidded.

"Why are you always so down on my hunches? I do go by gut feelings a lot," Joe said. "And you have to admit, they're hardly ever wrong." He started up the steps to Paula West's trailer.

"Right. And you're so modest about it," Frank teased. "Okay, you win. Let's get ready to join the dead. Or is it the undead?"

As Joe reached for the door, Frank noticed

that it had opened slightly. To his surprise, an arm emerged.

It was clutching a knife!

"Watch out!" Frank lunged forward to knock Joe out of the way.

Too late. As Frank shouted in rage and fear, the knife was plunged into Joe's chest!

Chapter 3

"JOE!" Frank watched the knife plunge to the hilt. He ran to catch his brother as he fell.

To Frank's amazement, Joe's shocked expression turned to one of relief, and then he started to laugh. Slowly Joe stepped back, revealing the retractable knife that had been pressed against him.

Frank released the breath he had been holding and wiped the sweat from his forehead as a blond woman with clear blue eyes stepped out of the trailer, examining the knife in the sunlight.

"I perfected this baby this morning," she said, pressing the knife against her other palm to demonstrate how the blade slid into the handle when pressed against an object. It created the perfect illusion of a blade piercing someone's skin—much better than the dime-store varieties.

"I'm Paula West." The woman put the knife in her shirt pocket. "You two must be the extra zombies Shane ordered. Come on in and let me change those handsome faces into decaying ghoul flesh."

Paula turned back into the trailer. Frank put a hand over his chest. His heartbeat was finally slowing to normal.

"Isn't she cool?" Joe said, eagerly following Paula through the door.

"Yeah," Frank grumbled. "She's almost as funny as the black plague."

Frank followed Joe into the trailer. The living room and kitchen area were full of boxes overflowing with latex masks, body parts, and prosthetic limbs wired to remote-control boxes to move the fake appendages.

Paula led Frank and Joe on a zigzag path through the equipment. "Please excuse the mess," she said. "By the time I get this place organized, the shoot will be over."

Finally they arrived at a room with two chairs positioned in front of a huge mirror. "Take a seat," she said.

"Why are you doing two extras' makeup?" Frank wanted to know.

"On a picture this small we all do everything," she said.

Frank and Joe sat down, watching Paula roll a cart out from the corner of the room and place it between the chairs. On the cart were several vials of makeup. She picked up a box of gray Pan-Cake makeup. "You guys are with the security team, right? I saw you on the set yesterday," Paula said.

Frank realized then that everyone on the set must know or have figured out who they were. Their work was going to be tougher than either they or Mr. Gold had hoped. "Kind of," Frank said. "Our dad is head of security. We came along to keep him company. It turned out that Shane Katz needed a few more extras for the zombie scene, so he asked us to be in the movie."

"Oh, yeah?" Paula sounded unconvinced. "So your being in the film has nothing to do with investigating Andrew Warmouth's murder?"

"No," Joe said. "Katz just needed some extra bodies. Besides, we leave murder investigations to the police."

"I see," Paula said, wetting a sponge.

She dabbed the small sponge into the makeup and stepped toward Joe. "I think I'll start with you," she said, applying the gray makeup to Joe's cheek.

"After I cover your face and hands with this, I'll apply black fake fingernails over your real fingernails. After that, I'll finish up with a couple of cuts on your face. The cuts will be small strips of latex that I apply with an adhesive called spirit gum. You shouldn't have to worry about any of this running off you when you sweat."

Frank watched as Paula skillfully applied the makeup. After graying Joe's features, she ran black lipstick over his lips.

"Were you very close to Warmouth?" Frank asked.

"What do you mean?" Paula retorted, continuing her work.

"I was just thinking that it must really be hard for any of you to have to work the day after he was killed," Frank said.

"It's not that bad," said Paula. "Warmouth and I never talked much. Ours was strictly a business relationship."

Frank hoped he wasn't being too obvious about pumping Paula for information. "Who do you think could have killed him?" Frank asked.

Paula shrugged. "Beats me. In this business you make enemies sometimes, and Warmouth wasn't a very easy person to get along with. I can think of a dozen or so people on the set who have probably wanted to make him disappear at one time or another. But as for who could have given in to the urge, I don't have the faintest idea."

Frank was amazed at how casually Paula discussed Warmouth's brutal murder. He made a mental note to discuss this with Joe later.

Paula held up a rubber scar for Joe to see. "I'm going to apply this to your cheek with solvent. After I add a little fake blood to it, it'll look like you have a hole in your cheek. Fake teeth will finish you up."

"Slick!" Joe exclaimed.

Paula finally pronounced Joe finished. Frank eyed his brother and groaned inside. He dreaded his own transformation. Ignoring him, Paula began applying the makeup to his face.

"I thought your assistant would make our faces up," Joe said, studying his own gruesome reflection in the mirror.

You mean you *hoped* her assistant would make us up, Frank thought. His brother was hopeless when it came to a pretty girl.

"I like to put my own personal signature on these zombie jobs," Paula said. "That's how I got my start, you know. *Attack of the Mutant Radioactive Zombies*. Now, *that* was a classic. Besides, I like to get my hands dirty, and Cathleen is still in training."

"I'm a big fan of yours," Joe said. "I've seen every movie you've worked on. *Radioactive Zombies* is my favorite."

"Ah, a fan!" Paula continued to apply the makeup to Frank's face. "Well, look around, if you're interested."

"Thanks," Joe said, leaving his chair.

"My brother tells me that you not only do horror makeups, but you also specialize in mechanical body parts for horror movies," Frank said.

"That's right. Fully functional moving heads or limbs have been around for a while, but I came up with a system that costs one-third of the standard cost to produce. I also think my creations are a little more sophisticated. Let's say, for instance, that I needed a mechanical head that looked like you. I'd make a cast of your face and fill it with a latex compound. The mask I'd made would look just like you. I'd stretch the mask over a mechanical head. Trigger wires work various parts of it just as human nerves do. I could raise your eyebrows, make you smile, even roll your eyes—and at a fraction of the usual rate."

"That's really something," Frank said.

Paula added a slash to Frank's throat, using a patch similar to the one she'd applied to Joe.

"All finished," Paula announced. "Let's go see what—Joe—is that right?"

"Oh," Frank said, standing up. "We didn't introduce ourselves. I'm Frank Hardy, and the guy snooping around your stuff is my brother, Joe."

"Let's go see what he's up to," Paula said.

They walked into the kitchen, where Joe was staring into a glass bowl containing a green, milky liquid.

"Get away from that!" Paula shouted.

Joe jumped back, startled.

Paula marched over to the bowl. "Would you

like to know what you almost stuck your nose in?"

Joe nodded, reddening in embarrassment. Paula took a fake hand off the counter next to the bowl. "This is a rubber hand. Observe," she said, dropping the hand into the bowl. There was a sizzling sound, and then the hand began to dissolve.

"Ouch!" Joe said.

"I use real sulfuric acid when someone in this movie is killed by the flask of acid the Reaper keeps on his belt. Prosthetics are tougher than human flesh. You have to use the real thing for it to be effective. When someone has acid thrown on him in the movie, we shoot a separate scene in which I pour acid on the fake limbs."

"Sorry," Joe said.

"You must have been a chemist to work in your field," Frank commented.

"As a matter of fact, I am," Paula replied.

"Really?" Frank looked surprised. "I was only kidding."

"Paula," Joe said before she could answer Frank, "I just remembered an article I read about you in *Gore* magazine a couple of years ago. It quoted you as saying that you didn't like the movies Warmouth produced. You said you would work only on traditional horror movies, not the kind of slasher films Warmouth produced. What made you change your mind about working with him?"

Paula's expression was cold. Then almost instantly a smile reappeared, but it seemed to be faked. She definitely had lost patience with the detectives and their questions.

"You guys had better go now. Katz doesn't like his scenes being held up, especially by extras. Go to the wardrobe trailer and get fitted before you report to the set."

Frank realized Joe had pushed the wrong button. He led the way to wardrobe, where the brothers quickly changed into ghoulish costumes. As they walked toward the house, Frank glanced at Joe. He could have just crawled out of a grave.

"I hate to say it," Joe said, "but I think Paula West just made our suspect list. She didn't seem upset about Warmouth's murder at all."

"You're telling me," Frank said. "And didn't she create the scythe for this movie?"

"Yeah, but the one used for most of the scenes is rubber. The real one was confiscated by Thornall this morning. Pinning Paula for the murder just because she designed the weapon might be kind of thin, but her attitude toward Warmouth does make her suspicious."

The crew was setting up for an outside shot in front of the house. Half a dozen other people in zombie makeup had gathered nearby. A crowd of onlookers gawked excitedly from behind a wooden barrier as Clervi walked out of the house in his Reaper costume. Clervi wore a dark hooded robe. His face was skeletal, and his gnarled, bony hands were gripping a scythe, which looked incredibly real to Frank.

Frank shuddered. How could a wimpy guy like Clervi appear to be so frightening?

While the camera and sound equipment was being set up in front of the porch, Frank watched Katz approach Clervi and begin talking to him. Frank strained to hear what the director was saying, but was interrupted by a man in his late twenties, dressed in a tank top and khaki pants.

"Hello," the tall man with dusty brown hair and dark eyes said, extending his hand to Frank. "I'm Mike Sinnochi, Shane's assistant."

The three of them exchanged introductions. "Do you know what you're going to do here, guys?" Mike asked.

"Not really," Frank replied.

"I haven't gotten my script yet," Joe said.

Mike laughed. "No problem. This scene takes place at night. The Reaper has lost control over you zombie slaves, and you attack your master, forcing him into the house. Got it so far?"

"Yeah," Frank said. "But if the scene takes place at night, how can you shoot it in the afternoon?"

"We're using a filtered lens on the camera that will make it appear to be night. It's called day for night," Mike explained.

"That's what I thought," Joe said, acting like an expert.

"So," Mike continued, "the zombies drive the Reaper toward the house. The Reaper, in retaliation, will pull his flask of acid from the pouch at his belt and fling streams of it at you. The acid, of course, is only tap water. Paula will come in later to fix things so zombies will appear to be dissolving in the acid. In fact, you guys may be called back later for close-ups."

Great, Frank thought. Then he noticed Shane Katz heading in their direction.

"Act lively, here comes the boss," Mike whispered.

"Hello, boys. Did Mike explain the shot to you?" Katz asked.

"Yep, I filled them in," Mike said, turning away to take care of something else.

"Do you have any idea how to do this scene?" Katz asked.

"I do." Joe began to drag his feet in a hypnotic march. He extended his arms straight ahead and put a blank expression on his face.

"Excellent, Joe," Katz said. "Frank, follow your brother's lead."

Frank imitated Joe, wondering if his flame red face was visible through the makeup. Katz observed them for a few minutes, then applauded.

"You guys are terrific," Katz said. "And Paula did an A-plus job on your makeup. I'll tell you what, I want you guys to lead the zombie pack."

"Cool!" Joe exclaimed.

Why not? Frank wondered. How much worse could things get?

Frank and Joe followed Katz over to the set, where the extras had been arranged. Clervi stood on the front porch, directly facing Frank and Joe, who were on the grass, the rest of the zombies in lines behind them.

"Quiet on the set," Frank heard Katz say. "Camera rolling—action!"

Frank and Joe shuffled slowly toward Clervi.

"Back, you ungrateful worm food!" Clervi shouted in a booming, theatrical voice.

Frank and Joe continued their slow march.

"None may touch the person of the Reaper!" Clervi cried. He reached into his pouch and pulled out the flask. He opened it and held it up in a threatening manner. "Back, you disobedient dogs! Back, I say!"

Clervi tossed a stream of liquid in Frank's direction. It landed on the lawn in front of his feet. Frank heard the crackling sound of something burning and glanced down. The grass, where the supposed tap water was thrown, was charred black. Clervi was throwing real acid.

Frank raised his eyes just in time to see Clervi aim the flask at Joe's face!

Chapter 4

THE CROWD OF ONLOOKERS screamed as Frank shot forward and raised his arm to knock the flask from Clervi's hand and away from all of them.

Joe stumbled backward and fell to the ground. His eyes wide, he glared at Frank, who was shoving Clervi back onto the porch with the force of a well-aimed karate kick.

"*Cut!*" Joe heard Katz shout. "What's going on here?"

"Yeah, Frank," Joe grumbled as Frank gripped his outstretched hand to help him up. "Why'd you knock into Clervi and then kick him?"

As the fans booed and hissed, Katz marched over to Joe and Frank. "Gentlemen, I appreciate creativity as much as the next man," he said through gritted teeth, "but this scene doesn't require any ad-libbing."

"Look at that," Frank demanded, pointing at the lawn where the flask had landed.

Joe saw the grass was totally charred where the flask had spilled its contents. "Someone filled that flask with real acid!" Joe said.

Katz was eyeing Clervi suspiciously. Clervi had dropped his hood, and even through his latex makeup, Joe could see how shaken the actor was. His eyes were terrified.

"I have no idea how that happened," Clervi insisted before any accusation was made.

"You'd better save your story for Sheriff Thornall, Matt," Katz said.

"You have to believe me, Shane. I don't even fill the flask. I'm not allowed to. My props weren't sitting on my table today as they usually are," Clervi said, wringing his hands.

"Where were they?" Joe asked.

"I walked over to Paula's trailer and saw my stuff on a table. I assumed Paula forgot to bring it to me, so I just took it."

"Who applied your makeup today?" Frank asked.

"Paula sends Cathleen to my trailer."

Katz's expression remained stern. "I took Paula to lunch today," he said to the Hardys. "I picked her up at her trailer at about eleven-thirty, after I got back from Dallas. I had to wait while she arranged Matt's stuff for him. I clearly remember seeing her fill that flask with tap water."

"There has to be some mistake," Clervi pleaded. "There must have been another flask in her trailer with acid in it, and she got them mixed up. It had to have been a mistake. I would never intentionally hurt anyone. Please, Shane, you have to believe me."

"Could there have been a mix-up?" Joe asked Katz.

"Anything's possible," Katz said. "There's a chance that Paula got the flasks confused. I still think Thornall should be notified, though." He raised his voice so the crew could hear. "I want everyone away from here until Thornall arrives. We're going to have to postpone this scene."

Katz turned to Clervi. "You'd better stay with me, Matt. I'm sure Thornall will want to talk to you."

Clervi groaned pitifully and began to peel the latex from his face.

Frank turned to Joe. "Let's get cleaned up and find Dad," he murmured. "I want him to run some background checks on our suspects."

Joe and Frank walked toward their trailer. "Why would Clervi want Warmouth dead? You don't bite the hand that feeds you," Frank said.

"I'm finding it hard to believe myself," Joe said. "If you want to commit murder, you don't do it in front of a crew of people with a flask of acid that you picked up when no one was around. Whoever killed Warmouth evidently wants this production to stop."

"I think someone wants *us* out of the way," Frank said. "The acid was aimed directly at us."

Joe shook his head. "I think that was a coincidence. I think someone wants the body count to grow until the film is canned. The person either has it in for Clervi or has something to gain by making the *Horror House* series fold."

Frank shook his head. "It doesn't make sense to me," he said. "Our list of suspects includes the star of the film, the special-effects and makeup coordinator, and her assistant. If the production is stopped, these people are out of work."

"Hey, you guys, wait up!" Joe heard a voice call from behind. Mike Sinnochi was running to catch up to them.

"Are you two okay?" Mike asked, winded.

"Yeah," Frank said. "We're fine."

Mike shook his head. "It's getting hairy around here. Do you guys have any leads yet?"

"What do you mean?" Joe asked.

"Shane said you were investigating Warmouth's murder. He told all of us to cooperate with you."

Joe fumed. Katz should have known better than to let everyone in on their investigation. If the killer hadn't known who they were before, he would definitely know by now.

"Well," Frank said, "since you know what we're doing, how'd you like to answer a few questions?"

"Sure," he said.

"Did you see or hear anything unusual the night of Warmouth's murder?" asked Frank.

"No," Mike said. "We wrapped up the bathtub of blood scene, then Shane called it a night. He asked me to go to the Mid-Way Café and get him a burger. When I got back, I went into his trailer and found him asleep in bed. I thought about waking him up before his food got cold, but he was dead to the world, so I let him rest. I went to bed in the trailer I'm sharing with a few other crew members. About fifteen minutes later I heard Cathy scream."

"Did you notice anything unusual this morning?" Joe asked.

"No," Mike replied. "Everything was calm, considering."

"Thanks, Mike," Frank said. "If you'll excuse us, we're going to find Paula and have her tell us how to get this mess off our faces."

"Oh, that's easy," Mike said. "Use lukewarm water to loosen the solvent on the rubber patches. Hand soap will take the makeup off." He grinned. "I've helped Paula before when she was shorthanded."

Joe and Frank thanked Mike again, then headed into their trailer.

Forty-five minutes later, when Joe and Frank

stepped out of the trailer, they were back to their former selves. "Amazing how long it takes to get clean," Joe remarked to his brother. "Now, what's the plan?"

"I think we should question Cathleen Bowley," Frank replied.

"Sounds good to me," Joe said, grinning.

As they started toward the makeup special-effects trailer, they spotted Cathleen walking up the front steps of Horror House. Joe nudged Frank and motioned for him to follow.

On the front porch Joe saw Sheriff Thornall speaking to Clervi. The sheriff was clutching a clear plastic bag that held the empty flask.

"I'd haul you in right now if Mr. Gold wasn't pulling strings for you," Joe heard Thornall say to the actor, who was cornered against the outside wall of the house like a frightened rabbit.

"I sincerely doubt that you were on a scenic tour of Beaufort at twelve o'clock at night when Warmouth was killed," Thornall growled. "This acid stunt may have been an accident, Clervi, but I'm warning you—I'm going to keep my eyes on you. If you have anything you want to share with me, you'd better tell me now."

"I've told you everything I know, Sheriff," Clervi pleaded.

"I've got enough on you already as it is. Come clean with me, and things might go easier on you," Thornall said.

"But I've told you the truth," Clervi insisted.

Thornall looked disgusted. "Fine, if that's the way you want it. I'm going to have the boys at the crime lab examine the flask. Don't run off anywhere, mister. I might be back very soon with a warrant for your arrest." Thornall turned and strode off to his patrol car past the few onlookers.

As Frank and Joe watched, Clervi slunk meekly away toward his trailer, his shoulders hunched forward, his head down.

"Sheriff," Joe called.

Thornall paused, saw the boys, and tilted his hat away from his eyes.

"What do you boys want?" Thornall asked impatiently as Joe and Frank caught up with him.

"We saw Paula West this afternoon. She acted very suspicious when we asked her about Warmouth," Joe said.

"So what?" Thornall grunted.

"It's possible she could have substituted the acid for tap water," Frank said.

"Katz vouched for Miss West. The only ones who could have switched the water are Clervi or Bowley. Maybe the two of them are in cahoots."

"Even if Clervi did kill Warmouth, why would he toss acid at the extras? That would be insane," Joe insisted.

"Who said he was sane?" Thornall said.

"Sheriff," Frank said, "don't you think there's a possibility that Clervi's being set up?"

"Now, look," Thornall said, "I've had enough of your kindergarten speculation. You wet-nosed pups stay out of my way, or you'll end up with Clervi when I toss him in the cell." With that Thornall stormed to his car.

"I thought that went well," Joe said sarcastically. "I thought we were going to work together. Guess he just meant Dad, not us." Clearly, Thornall had decided Clervi was guilty and didn't want anyone to confuse him with contrary evidence. Joe realized it was possible that Clervi might really be guilty, but the possibility of sending an innocent man to prison made him shudder.

"Let's find Cathleen Bowley," Frank said in a similar state of confusion.

When Joe and Frank entered Horror House, they found Cathleen sitting on a sofa in the living room, reading a magazine.

"Miss Bowley," Frank said.

Cathleen raised her eyes from her reading and smiled. "What can I do for you?"

"We were wondering if we could ask you a few questions about the night Warmouth was killed," said Frank.

"Could you tell us what you were doing and how you came upon the body?" Joe asked very politely.

"Okay. Let's see. I'd just helped Paula put

away a few things after the bathtub of blood scene," Cathleen began, folding the magazine and putting it aside. "I went for a walk outside to relax before going to bed. It was dark, and no one else was around. I walked past the house and noticed that the door was open. I was wide awake and decided to heat up a cup of milk to help me sleep. I stepped into the hallway, found Warmouth's body—and screamed. The crew came running, and I just freaked out. I see gory things in my line of work all the time, but I'd never seen a real dead body before."

Cathleen shuddered at the memory. "I don't ever want to see one like that again."

Frank waited for her to calm down. Then he asked, "How well did you know Warmouth?"

"Not well at all. This is the first production for Fourteen Karat Studios I've worked on."

"You didn't notice anyone else that night?" Joe asked.

"Not a soul, except Mike," Cathleen replied. "I saw him step out of Shane's trailer and walk toward his own."

"Were you in the special-effects trailer this morning?" Frank asked.

"I ducked in for a moment to grab some stuff."

"How long were you with Matt?" asked Joe.

"Oh, about an hour, I guess," Cathy replied.

"Was Matt there the whole time?" Frank asked.

"No. He left for about fifteen minutes. He said he had to make an urgent phone call."

"Did he seem nervous or uncomfortable to you?" asked Frank.

"He always seems that way," Cathy said, smiling.

"Thanks a lot for your time," Frank said.

"No problem." Cathy smiled sadly, then went back to her magazine.

Joe and Frank left the house. "Let's head for Dad's trailer. I'm surprised he hasn't caught wind of the acid incident and come looking for us yet," Frank said.

"What do you think about Cathleen?" Joe asked.

Frank shrugged. "I'd like Dad to run a background check on her. It is procedure, right?"

Joe nodded, but he thought that checking her out would be a waste of time. He had a gut feeling Cathleen would come up clean.

"You know, Joe," said Frank thoughtfully, "if we're pretty sure that Cathy is clean and that Clervi is being set up, then our main suspect has to be Paula West. Both incidents had special-effects equipment involved. Aside from Cathy, who has no reason that we know of to murder Warmouth, Paula is the only other person with access to the scythe and to acid."

"Yeah, but evidently she doesn't lock up her trailer. Clervi walked in and took his props while she was eating with Katz," Joe said.

"Then what you're saying is that anyone could have stepped into the trailer and switched the water," Frank concluded.

"Yep," Joe said. "And there are at least thirty people on this set."

"I wonder if Dad can get hold of Paula's contract with Fourteen Karat Studios. Maybe we can find out what would motivate her to work for someone she evidently dislikes," Frank said.

"Maybe Gold can give Dad some paperwork on Paula," suggested Joe. "I think we should also take a trip to the nearest library and dig up some background on the house itself. We might be missing something that's totally unrelated to the film. Maybe Warmouth's death was caused by someone who isn't on the crew."

"Good idea," Frank said. "We also have to consider those fans who line the fence around this place. Maybe we should question some of them."

Joe and Frank reached their father's trailer. Joe had his hand raised to knock on the door when the sound of a strange voice coming from inside stopped him.

"You better mark my words, outsider!" a husky voice shouted. "What happened to Warmouth could happen to you!"

Joe spun toward Frank.

Someone was threatening their father!

Chapter 5

"DAD!" Joe charged into Fenton's trailer with Frank one step behind. Fenton and a man in his mid-sixties were startled out of their chairs at the small dining table.

"Is everything all right?" Frank demanded. "Was someone threatening you?"

"No, boys, everything's fine. What you heard was just a very passionate warning." Fenton motioned for them to all sit down. "Come here, there's someone I want you to meet."

Frank and Joe took seats.

"This is Harold Hughes, the owner of the house."

"You must use your influence to stop the filming, Mr. Hardy," Harold Hughes said, cutting off Fenton. "I know who's responsible for the murder."

"Who are you talking about, Mr. Hughes?" Frank asked.

Hughes leaned close to Frank and Joe, his eyes wide. "The house," he whispered. "The spirits trapped in my home don't take kindly to the gory trash Warmouth was responsible for. When my wife and I signed the deal with Warmouth, we thought he was going to tell the truth. Instead, he's made a mockery of those ancient powers. Finally the spirits will avenge this evil transgression."

Frank glanced at Joe, then at Fenton, who had obviously been humoring the man. Frank turned back to Harold Hughes, who was pointing a finger at him.

"You are a disbeliever," Hughes muttered. "You are blind to the supernatural presence that hangs over this property. Warmouth was a disbeliever, too. And you know what happened to him. You have to get these people away from my house."

"Mr. Hughes," Joe said, "if the ghosts in your house are responsible for this, why did they wait until the fifth movie to do something about it?"

"Ah, yes," Hughes said, smiling like a vulture. "They've kept quiet until now. But believe me, the spirits will abide these films no longer. The spirits never wanted to hurt anyone, but now they realize the bloody course they must take to have peace again."

"If these spirits are so upset, why do they allow you and Mrs. Hughes to live with them?" Frank asked.

"Because we respect them," Hughes said. "It is suspected that our house was built on a Native American burial ground. When we discovered the spirits' presence, we wrote a book about them, sharing our discovery of life after death with the entire world. We were foolish, though, to agree to these movies. We've had to hire a security man to keep people off our property. They come year-round to see the house where the Reaper movies are made."

"Did you ever try to talk to Warmouth about this?" Fenton asked.

Harold Hughes stood up abruptly. "I have to go back to the hotel," he said, going to the door. He paused with his hand on the knob. "Warmouth was just the beginning," he said ominously. "Leave, before others are hurt."

He left, slamming the door behind him.

"That guy is crazy," Joe said, turning to Fenton. "What was that all about?"

"Harold knows Sheriff Thornall. It seems that Thornall told him all about Warmouth's murder," Fenton explained.

"If Harold resents people exploiting the house, then why did he rent it to Warmouth in the first place?" Frank wondered.

"I think Harold is more upset with the way

his story has been portrayed than with its being told. Warmouth took a story of a haunted house and turned it into a story about a superhuman maniac who frequently returns from the dead to hack up teenagers who rent the house," Joe said.

"Do you think he would be upset enough to kill?" Frank said.

Joe shrugged. "He isn't one of the crew, but it is his house. He has security clearance and can come and go as he pleases. Let's check him out later and see what he was doing at the time of the murder."

"How did the filming go?" Fenton asked.

"You didn't hear about the excitement this afternoon?" Joe said.

"I've spent the last two hours listening to Harold Hughes rant. What did I miss?"

Frank filled his father in on everything, including his suspicions of Paula West.

"Things are heating up," Fenton said, shaking his head. "I want you two to watch your backs. If someone is trying to jinx this film with accidents, it means anyone could get hurt at any time. It does seem as though someone could be trying to frame Clervi, but let's not discount him as a suspect. He may want us to think he's being set up so we won't finger him. I'll go to Thornall's office and run those background checks."

"Joe and I want to go to the library in Fort

Worth to check on articles about Horror House," Frank said. "That is, if you have enough guards here."

Fenton nodded.

"Let's check out the library later and grab something to eat now," Joe suggested. "I want to see if any more scenes are being shot later."

"Good idea," Frank said. "I didn't know it was so late. Want to join us, Dad?"

"I think I'll get those background checks under way. I'll also give Gold a call to see if he can add any extra information about the suspects. I'll eat later."

Frank and Joe left Fenton's trailer in time to see the catering truck pull up to the house. Men in white uniforms pulled silver trays loaded with food from the truck and carried them into the house.

"Now, that's what I call service," Joe said, making a beeline for the house. "No Mid-Way Café for Joe Hardy tonight."

Frank followed Joe, the sight of food reminding him that he had missed lunch.

After dinner Frank and Joe stepped out on the front porch to decide what to do next. Frank watched as an exterior shot was being set up in the same spot as the earlier zombie sequence. Already a small crowd of fans had gathered.

"They're getting ready to do our scene again,"

Joe said. "We'd better get over to makeup. I can't believe no one told us about this."

"Before you call your agent to complain," Frank said, "I think you ought to know they're filming a different scene."

"How do you know?" Joe asked.

"I talked to Mike Sinnochi in the dining room while you were going back for seconds," Frank replied. "Mike also told me that the Fort Worth library is open until eight o'clock, so we have plenty of time to hit it tonight if we want to."

"Good. We'll head over there after this scene. Which one are they doing, anyway?"

"The Reaper is going out to attack a mailman outside the house," Frank explained.

"Wait a minute," Joe said. "He did the same thing to a milkman in the last movie."

"That's why they're called formula movies," Frank chuckled. "If a proven formula works once, why change it?"

Frank watched as Clervi, in full costume, appeared on the set. An actor wearing a postal uniform appeared next.

"That's the same guy who played the milkman in the last movie!" Joe exclaimed.

Katz arrived, carrying a coffee cup in one hand. Frank noticed that Paula West and Cathleen Bowley were also on the set.

A full twenty minutes was devoted to setting the camera in its proper place and lowering the microphone on a boom over Clervi's head.

Frank watched as Thornall's patrol car pulled into the driveway. Thornall stepped out of the car, closed the door, then sat on the hood of his car, silently watching Clervi.

Frank turned his attention back to the set and saw Paula West check Clervi's makeup and props. Clervi, who was holding the Reaper's scythe, glanced over at Thornall. Though Frank couldn't get a good look at Clervi's face, he knew Thornall's sudden appearance, after remarking that he might return with a warrant, was making Clervi shake in his Reaper boots.

Frank heard Katz's voice boom out. "Okay, people. It's almost sunset. Because of the accident earlier, we have to put the mailman scene in the can tonight. We have one hour of light remaining, so let's get it right."

Katz walked back behind the camera and sat in his director's chair.

"Places, everyone," Katz called.

Clervi assumed his position behind a bush. The actor portraying the mailman stood on the sidewalk ten feet in front of the bush.

"Roll camera," Katz said.

Frank heard the camera come to life as the camera operator bent his head to the viewfinder.

"Action!" Katz commanded.

Frank watched as the mailman strolled up the sidewalk, whistling and going through a pile of envelopes that he'd pulled from his pouch. As the man approached the bush, Clervi leapt in front of the mailman, blocking his route.

The mailman screamed and stumbled backward.

"I've got a first-class delivery for you, human!" Clervi shouted, waving the scythe in the air.

"The Reaper has a wicked sense of humor," Joe whispered in Frank's ear.

Frank watched as Clervi swung the scythe at the mailman. As the scythe closed in on the actor, Clervi abruptly pulled it back. The mailman was obviously confused. Clervi tried to swing the scythe once more, but pulled it back again.

"Cut!" Frank heard Katz scream.

Katz walked over to Clervi. "We're losing daylight, Matt. What's wrong with you?" Katz demanded.

"I'm sorry, Shane. I'm just so upset about everything that's been happening, I can't pull myself together," Clervi said, dropping the scythe to the ground.

"Be a professional, Matt. We're all under a lot of strain," Katz said.

Clervi pointed toward Thornall, then whispered something to Katz.

"Don't worry about him," Katz insisted. "If he had enough proof, he'd have hauled you in this afternoon."

Katz picked up the scythe. "Now, watch how I do this, then let's put this scene to bed."

Katz swung the scythe at the mailman. The

scythe struck the mailbag the actor was carrying. As Katz pulled the scythe away, Frank heard a loud ripping sound and saw envelopes pour out of the bag.

The bag was ripped practically in two.

The scythe was real!

Chapter 6

"HOLD IT!" Frank ran up to the director, Joe on his heels. Katz hadn't noticed the mailbag because he'd already raised the scythe to strike at the actor again.

"Wait!" Frank reached out and caught the handle of the scythe before it could come down on the actor.

"What do you think you're doing?" Katz exclaimed.

"You could have killed him! This scythe is real!" Frank shouted, pointing at the torn mailbag.

Katz glanced down at the envelopes on the sidewalk, his eyes wide with alarm. "I was looking at Matt. I had no idea . . ." Katz said, his voice trailing off, his gaze fixed on Clervi.

"I think I've created a monster," Katz muttered, fearfully backing away from Clervi.

Clervi ripped at the latex on his face as he tried to stammer an explanation. No words came. He buried his face in his hands.

Sheriff Thornall stepped up next to Frank. "I'll take that, thank you." Thornall snatched the scythe from Frank's hands.

"Listen up," Thornall announced to the crew. "I'm confiscating everything on this set that could be used to hurt anyone. I want every sharp instrument and every chemical from the special-effects trailer. I want you folks to know that I plan to be on the set constantly from this night on. I will be present for every scene filmed."

Frank noticed that Paula West had worked her way through the crew. She approached Thornall. "If you take my equipment, I won't be able to do my job," Paula protested to Thornall.

"I only want the harmful substances, Miss West, like this scythe and the acid you keep. By the way," Thornall said, running his finger down the edge of the scythe, "how many of these overgrown razors do you have?"

"We had three, until you confiscated the first one," Paula said. "If you take this one, that'll leave us with one. And if it gets broken, we won't have a backup."

"I'm going to have to ask you to turn over the other one," Thornall said.

"This scene called for the rubber scythe," Katz interjected. "Someone evidently substituted the real one,'' Katz added, glancing at Clervi. ''We use the real scythe only for scenes where the Reaper is striking an inanimate object, such as a door.''

''Did you give Mr. Clervi his scythe, Miss West?'' Frank asked Paula.

''I'll handle the questioning,'' Thornall growled, glaring at Frank. ''Let's step inside.'' Thornall took Clervi by the arm, steering him up onto the front porch of the house. Thornall paused at the doorway. ''Hang around, Miss West,'' he said to Paula. ''When I'm finished questioning the Reaper here, I'll be heading to your trailer to ask you some more questions and to pick up the dangerous items.''

With Clervi in tow, Thornall entered the house.

As the disgruntled crowd of onlookers began to disperse, Frank glanced at the actor playing the mailman. The man was studying the tear in the mailbag.

''Are you okay?'' Frank asked.

The actor nodded, then walked away, his face pale and eyes wide.

''I'm calling it a night,'' Katz announced. ''I don't care about our schedule. Everyone just relax tonight.''

Frank watched as Paula stormed over to Katz.

''Doesn't he need a warrant to seize my equipment?'' Paula said to Katz. ''This isn't right. I need everything that's in my trailer in order to work."

"Just cooperate with him, Paula," Katz said. "It's for the best."

Paula West rushed off toward her trailer, sidestepping Frank and Joe, who wanted to question her.

"We need to ask you some questions, Miss West," Frank called after her.

"Later!" she shouted over her shoulder. "If you want to interrogate me, take a number behind the sheriff!"

Katz stood beside the Hardys, shaking his head. "I have to call Leonard Gold to tell him about all this. We have a very large fly in our soup. I hope Thornall doesn't clean Paula's trailer out. That bumpkin may ruin this whole shoot. And the way things are going, I don't know whether to resent him or be eternally grateful."

"Mr. Katz," Joe asked, "could Clervi have picked up the real scythe by mistake? I mean, the acid incident could have been an accident, too."

"Yes," Katz admitted. "But I definitely wouldn't call what happened to Andy an accident. I've known Matthew for years, but now I'm beginning to think his role has affected his sanity. If you want my opinion, I think Clervi is responsible. As much as I hate to admit it, I almost hope Thornall takes him away."

"Things don't look good for him," Frank agreed. "But why would Clervi want to kill Warmouth?"

"Do insane people need reasons?" Katz asked. "Maybe a voice in his head told him to do it. Now, if you'll excuse me, I want to check in with Mr. Gold."

Katz headed for his trailer, leaving the Hardys alone on the lawn.

"Do you want to go watch Thornall question Clervi?" Joe asked.

"No," Frank replied. "He'd just shoo us away. He'd claim we're interfering with his investigation."

"So now what?" Joe said.

"Well, we aren't going to sit around and twiddle our thumbs. I think we might have just enough time to check out the library," Frank said.

Frank and Joe sat at the microfilm machine, relieved that they'd been lucky enough to find a helpful librarian who had escorted them to the machine, pulled all the available data on the Hughes house, and brought it to them. The librarian had explained to Frank that during the summer, when high schools were closed and colleges offered a limited number of summer courses, she had so much time on her hands that helping the Hardys came as a relief from boredom.

Frank operated the machine while Joe sat

next to him, reading over his shoulder. Frank scanned an old issue of the Fort Worth *Messenger*. At last he found an article on the Hughes house.

"This article was written before the Hugheses finished their book," Frank said. "It tells about the first haunting." Frank read through the article, then shook his head. "There's nothing here you haven't told me," he said to Joe, pulling the microfilm out and loading the next one.

The next article Frank scanned was filled with local speculation about what the papers were calling Horror House. Because a local banker had come forward and told the press that the Hugheses were in financial trouble, many people thought they were trying to hype their house in order to sell it.

Frank found a book review of the Hugheses' novel. It slammed the book, claiming that not only was the book boring and predictable, it never even got scary.

Another article announced the filming of a movie in Beaufort, Texas. The working title of the project was *The Hughes Encounter*. Harold and Kitty Hughes were overjoyed at the prospect of having their story put on the screen.

Next Frank read an article that was printed after the first film came out. The Hugheses were clearly unhappy with the final product, but a gag order in their contract didn't permit them to voice their objections to the press. The only comment Kitty Hughes issued was, "Let's just say it's not what we thought it would be."

The remaining articles focused less on the Hugheses than on the making of the films and the onslaught of fanatical fans to Beaufort each time an installment went into production.

Joe finished taking notes on a small notepad while Frank returned the microfilm to the librarian and thanked her. Then he and Joe left.

"Let's stop for a burger," Joe said as Frank pulled the car out of the library parking lot.

"Joe, you ate about two and a half hours ago," Frank said. He never ceased to be amazed by his brother's appetite.

"I know, but we missed lunch, and I'm used to my three square meals a day," Joe said, patting his stomach.

Frank gave in and stopped at a diner halfway to Beaufort.

It was almost ten when Frank pulled the car onto the Hugheses' property. Frank stopped beside the security gate near the end of the driveway. A guard stepped up to the window of the rented car.

"Hi, Eddie," Frank said as the bearded man in a security uniform bent down to peer into the car.

"Hey, guys. How's it going?" Eddie asked.

"Not bad." Frank glanced over Eddie's shoulder at the young fans still lined up outside the fence that surrounded most of the Hughes property. The fans were carrying burning candles and walking back and forth solemnly.

"What's with the groupies?" Joe asked Eddie.

"It's their own special service for Warmouth," Eddie said. "Warmouth's body is going to be sent back to Los Angeles tomorrow after the medical examiner finishes the autopsy. These folks are having a little memorial for him tonight."

"If anything goes wrong, give us a call," Joe offered.

"Thanks," Eddie said. "I'll do that."

Eddie walked back to the security booth and opened the gate for Frank. Frank saw several fans run toward the opening. Quickly he drove onto the property, then glanced back in the rearview mirror. No one had managed to slip in.

Frank parked the car in the gravel lot marked for the crew. As he and Joe walked toward Fenton's trailer, Frank noticed that the sky above was moonless. Frank thought he had never seen a night so dark.

Joe took out his penlight and lit the way so they wouldn't stumble over a rock or step into one of the mole burrows. Snakes came out at night to cool off, also, Frank reflected. He was aware that copperhead snakes, and even a few species of rattlesnakes, were common in these parts. He was glad Joe had the light.

Frank and Joe entered their father's trailer to

find Fenton sitting at the table, poring over some paperwork.

"Hello, guys," Fenton said. "Did you find anything?"

"Nothing really useful," Frank said. "We did find an article that described how unhappy the Hugheses were with the series. What did you find out?"

"The background checks came up clean," Fenton said. "Leonard Gold told me about the scythe incident, though, and while he was at it he gave me some information on Clervi and West. It seems Clervi had been trying to break his contract with Warmouth. He'd been offered a role in a serious movie and the filming coincided with the filming of *Horror House Five*. Warmouth refused to break the contract or postpone shooting."

"There's the motive we've been looking for," Joe said.

"What about Paula West?" Frank asked.

"According to Leonard Gold, she accepted the *Horror House* job at one-third her usual rate," Fenton said.

"Why would one of the most innovative people in the special-effects industry agree to work for less than her usual fee? Especially on a project that she didn't like?" Frank wondered.

"Maybe Warmouth had something on her," Joe suggested.

"It's possible," Fenton agreed.

"Getting back to the Hugheses, though," Frank said. "There's one thing that bothers me. Even though the *Horror House* movies are a success, the most recent articles suggest that the Hugheses are still near bankruptcy. If the films are so successful, why are the Hugheses so broke? Didn't they get paid for the rights to their story? One article said that during the filming of the third installment, the Hugheses even put the house up for sale, but no one would buy a haunted house. Why didn't Andrew Warmouth just buy it himself?"

"I think we should pay a visit to the hotel where the Hugheses are staying," Joe decided.

"All in good time," Fenton said, yawning. "You guys covered a lot of ground tonight. You'd better get some sleep so we can get an early start tomorrow."

Reluctantly Frank and Joe said good night to Fenton, then headed back to their own trailer. Frank realized just how hectic the day had been as he plodded sleepily up the front step after Joe. He could hardly stay awake long enough to get ready for bed.

He was about to collapse onto the bed when he noticed a shadow on the wall beside the door. He peered closer. The shadow was of someone in a flowing robe and hood.

It was the Reaper—raising his scythe!

Chapter 7

WITH A SHOUT, Frank lunged toward the dark figure. He clasped the Reaper's wrist and slammed it and the scythe against the wall.

He twisted the intruder around and smashed him against the front door. Joe had gotten up in time to watch the scythe fly from the Reaper's hand.

The hooded man fell to the floor as Frank's weight brought him down. Joe realized that Matthew Clervi—or someone dressed like the Reaper—must have been in the trailer before they entered.

"Get the scythe, Joe!" Frank commanded, pinning the struggling Reaper to the floor.

"Please, let me up!" came the muffled cry from under Frank. It was Clervi. "I wasn't going to hurt you! I just came to talk!"

Joe was at his brother's side, gripping the scythe and testing the blade.

"Frank," he said in a low voice, "it's plastic. Let him up."

Embarrassed, Frank released his grip on Clervi and slowly stood up. He extended a hand to the actor and hauled him to his feet. Clervi dusted himself off and pulled his hood away from his face.

"I didn't mean to startle you," Clervi said apologetically. "I just needed to talk to you. I feel it's important that you hear my side of the story."

"I'm sorry I jumped on you like that," Frank said. "With all these accidents going on, I guess I'm sort of edgy."

"It's my fault. I should have taken the time to change my clothes. I was just so afraid that Thornall would arrest me. I feel as if he's watching my every move. I don't know what I'm going to do," Clervi whined, nervously wringing his hands.

Joe felt sorry for the shaken Clervi, but he reminded himself that Clervi was an actor and Joe didn't want to be fooled by him. Too many signs were pointing to Clervi, and an objective detective could not ignore the evidence.

"Why are you still in your Reaper getup so late after the shoot?" Frank asked.

"I had to make a public appearance in Fort Worth this evening. I'm drumming up publicity for the video release of *Horror House Four*." His expression faltered. He reached out toward Frank. "You've got to help me! I'm innocent!" Clervi cried.

"We intended to talk to you," Joe said.

"I heard that you were part of security, and I also felt horrible about that acid scene. That's why I waited here for you. I wanted to assure you both that I had nothing to do with the accidents—or Warmouth's death," Clervi explained.

"Can you tell us where you were the night of Warmouth's murder?" Frank asked.

"I went for a drive. I was very upset because I'd been offered a role in a movie. It was from a play I did many years ago, and I've wanted to be in the film version for a long time. Many producers wouldn't consider me because of my work on the *Horror House* series. This particular producer, though, had seen me do the part on stage and knew I was right for the role," Clervi said.

"And you were upset because Warmouth wouldn't let you out of your contract to be in that movie?" Frank asked.

"Yes," Clervi replied. "I accepted the first Reaper role because I was struggling to make it as an actor, and I needed the work. At first, all the recognition was great. But now it seems as though my fame as the Reaper has worked against me. This dramatic movie was my opportunity to show the public that Matthew Clervi is more than a third-rate horror film star. But Warmouth was relentless in holding me to my contract. I was upset but not upset enough to murder him.''

''Where exactly did you go that night?'' Joe asked.

Clervi shook his head. ''I don't even know. I drove all through the back roads of Beaufort. I got lost at one point, and it took me a good half-hour to find my way back here. The roads in this town are mostly forest on either side.''

''Did anyone see you that night? Did you pass any other cars or people on the road?'' Frank asked.

''Not a soul,'' Clervi said. ''This town rolls up its sidewalks at nine o'clock. It was close to ten when I went for the drive.''

''So, there's no one who could vouch for you? Can you think of anyone on the set who may have seen you leave?'' Joe asked.

''It was dark when I left, and I didn't notice anyone,'' Clervi replied, grimacing. ''It's the truth, but I'm beginning to wonder if even I would believe me,'' Clervi added.

''What happened when you got back?'' Frank asked.

''I went to my trailer and began rereading the *Horror House* script. I heard the commotion outside a few minutes later,'' Clervi said.

''Did you notice anything or anyone out of

the ordinary when you returned to the set?'' Joe asked.

"No. Everyone seemed to be in their trailers, bedded down for the night," Clervi replied.

"Okay, we heard your explanation for the acid incident. Let's talk about what happened this evening, during the mailman sequence," Frank said.

"Well, when I picked up the scythe, I had no idea I was carrying a lethal weapon with me. The fake scythe looks so much like the real one, and it weighs the same. I could have killed someone with that thing," Clervi said.

"Katz almost did," Frank reminded Clervi.

"You guys have to do two things," Clervi pleaded. "You have to believe me, and you have to help me. Someone else is responsible for this. I'm being framed."

"We want to believe you, Mr. Clervi," Frank said. "Unfortunately, you have no proof where you were on the night of Warmouth's murder."

"Wait a minute," Clervi said, his eyes widening. "I have to keep a ledger for my rental car for the studio. It gives the date, destination, and mileage for every trip, to help out at tax time. I marked down everything that I did that night, and there's a considerable difference on the car mileage."

"That won't help," Frank said.

"What do you mean, it won't help?" Clervi argued.

"Frank's right, Mr. Clervi," Joe said. "You could have written those entries after the murder. And if no one saw you leave, you could have left the set at any time in the day. It wouldn't hold up in court."

"Then I'm done for," Clervi muttered, his last hope dashed. "I might as well turn myself in to Thornall and get it over with."

"Maybe we can think of something else, Mr. Clervi," Frank said.

"Please," Clervi said absently. "Call me Matt." Clervi's face suddenly lit up. "I have one more suggestion," he said. "What if you guys retraced my steps that night?"

"I don't think—" Frank began.

But Joe interrupted his brother. "Sure, Matt," he said. "We could give it a try."

Clervi would go mad with anxiety if he and Frank didn't at least try to help him, Joe thought. Besides, even though retracing Clervi's steps might seem like a waste of time, they might actually discover something. A person could find the most interesting things, Joe had learned, taking the side paths.

"Okay, Matt," Frank said. "We'll give it a try."

After changing, the Hardys with Clervi stepped out of the trailer and into the night. "My car's parked behind the house," Clervi said, leading Joe and Frank toward the house.

Horror House loomed ominously. Joe shivered. No wonder the Hugheses were convinced the place was haunted, he thought. From the front, in the darkness, the house resembled a hideous face—the door a grinning mouth and the two attic windows beady eyes. But wait—was it his imagination, or did Joe see a shadow move past a window on the first floor?

"I think someone's in the house," Joe announced, pausing to get a better look at the window.

"It's probably Shane," Clervi said. "He walks around the house at night for inspiration, or so he claims."

"Yeah, but with the lights off?" Joe wondered.

"Do you think we should check it out?" Frank asked.

"With a murderer on the loose, I don't think it would be a bad idea," Joe replied.

The Hardys and Clervi walked up on the porch, and Joe pushed the front door in as silently as he could.

"Why are you being so quiet?" Clervi whispered.

"What if Katz isn't in there? We might be sneaking up on the killer," Joe whispered back.

"I see your point," Clervi said, shuddering.

The Hardys and Clervi crept into the hallway. Joe felt for a light switch and flipped it on. Nothing happened.

"The electricity is off," Joe said.

"I know where the circuit breakers are," Clervi said. "They're down in the basement."

"Okay," Joe said, handing Clervi his penlight. "Take this."

"Be careful," Frank said. "Scream your head off if anything happens."

Joe heard Clervi slip away. The darkness was so thick he could barely see a foot in front of his face. Joe continued to creep forward. He assumed he was in the dining room. Just then Frank bumped into something.

"Are you okay?" Joe whispered over his shoulder.

"I'm fine," Frank whispered back.

Suddenly the lights burst on, and Joe saw Shane Katz. He was standing in the soaring, two-story dining room directly beneath a huge chandelier. Katz gave Joe a smile. "Thank goodness," he said. "I thought you were the killer."

Joe started to speak, but before he could get a single word out, he heard a tearing sound coming from above.

Joe raised his eyes.

The crystal chandelier over Katz's head was pulling loose, ready to plummet to the floor!

Chapter 8

JOE SPRANG FORWARD and caught Katz with his shoulder. The two of them flew to one side just as the chandelier crashed to the parquet floor. Joe shielded Katz with his body, burying his head between his arms as shards of glass rained down on them.

Slowly Joe lifted his head to look up at the gaping hole in the ceiling, two stories overhead, where the chandelier had been attached. He heard the sound of crunching glass and saw Frank precariously pick his way through the debris to them.

"Are you all right?" Frank asked, brushing glass off Joe's shirt.

"Yeah. Fine," Joe said, pulling himself up and giving a hand to Katz.

Katz exhaled deeply and stared at the Hardys. "You saved my life," he croaked. He was shuddering and his skin was pale and covered with sweat.

"What were you doing here?" Joe asked, helping Katz to his feet.

"I come here for inspiration," Katz replied. "And with the way things are going, I really needed it tonight. I was here in the dining room when the lights went out, so I decided to stay put until my eyes got used to the dark. I wasn't about to stumble and fall."

"Are you hurt?" Frank asked.

"No," Katz said, rubbing his head. "I'm just a bit shaken."

"Wait here while we check out where the chandelier was attached," Joe said to Katz. "Come on, Frank."

Joe headed up the stairway. On the second floor he noticed an attic door in the hall ceiling. Standing on tiptoes, Joe grasped the string that was hanging down from the door and unstrapped the foldable, wooden ladder that was attached to the inside of the door.

With Frank right behind him, Joe climbed up into the attic. When he stood at the top, Joe felt another string brush his face. He pulled it, and light flooded the immediate area, creating pockets of deep shadow along the walls.

The boards of the attic floor were brittle and splintery. Joe carefully stepped across the floor to the area above the dining room. He found the hole where the chandelier had pulled loose and examined the pulley through which a heavy cord had run to support the chandelier's weight. Joe glanced up and saw where the cord had been anchored to the inside of the roof. Next he and Frank examined a small electrical box that looked as if it powered a huge attic fan. A single electrical wire had been pulled from the box and wrapped around the cord.

"What do you make of this, Frank?" Joe said, pointing to the frayed cord.

"It looks like someone took a wire and stripped it—then wrapped the exposed wire around the cord," Frank explained. "When the electricity was turned on, the wire burned through the cord, loosening the tension on the pulley, and the chandelier fell, pulling some of the plaster free with it."

"Let's get back downstairs," Joe said.

Joe and Frank hurried down to the dining room to find Clervi had returned.

"You keep him away from me!" Katz shouted, pointing at Clervi. "He killed Warmouth, and he tried to kill me!"

"I don't know what you're talking about," Clervi insisted. "I didn't try to kill you."

"Then why did you happen to be here when the chandelier fell? You know I walk in the dining room when I'm here alone. I spend most of my time thinking of new scenes in this room.

You knew that! You could have easily planned this whole thing!'' Katz shouted.

''What took you so long?'' Frank asked Clervi.

''The circuit breakers are all the way in the basement. After I switched the breakers on and was coming back up, I dropped your penlight and went back down the stairs to look for it. It took me a few minutes to find it,'' Clervi explained.

''He's lying!'' Katz exclaimed. ''Can't you see? He engineered this whole thing!''

Joe heard the front door open. Paula West and Sheriff Thornall hurried inside. Joe could hear other people also. Several crew members were pressed up against the dining room entrance.

''I heard an awful noise,'' Paula said. ''Sheriff Thornall was making a night check on the set. I caught him before he drove away. What happened?''

''Well,'' Thornall said, staring at the chandelier, ''either you fellas were playing Tarzan on that thing, or there are some awful big termites in these walls.''

''Frank,'' Joe said, ''why don't you take Sheriff Thornall up to the attic and show him what we found?''

As Frank led the sheriff upstairs, Fenton arrived. Joe explained what had happened to his father and Paula.

"Well," Thornall interrupted Joe's story. "It looks like the Reaper has a full bag of tricks!"

Joe turned toward the booming voice and watched as the sheriff and Frank reentered the room.

Thornall strode up to Clervi and clasped the shaken actor's arm. "Time for another heart-to-heart." Thornall escorted Clervi out of the house. Joe shook his head as he watched the actor being led away.

Then Joe turned to Paula. "Where were you during all this, Miss West?" he asked.

"I was preparing a few things in my trailer," Paula replied. "I gave Cathy the night off before I realized how much work I had to finish before tomorrow morning."

"Why are you questioning her?" Katz interrupted. "It's obvious Clervi is the killer."

"Clervi has been with us for the last twenty minutes or so," Frank said.

"But he's been back from his public appearance for an hour," Paula said. "I saw him when his car pulled into the driveway."

"That would have given him time to rig the chandelier," Fenton said. "Look, you people had better get some rest. If you want my advice, Mr. Katz, don't take any more evening strolls through the house."

Joe followed Frank and Fenton outside.

"I was ready to believe that Clervi was being set up," Frank said. "Now I'm not so sure."

"I have to agree," Joe said. "Clervi does look awfully guilty. He may have led us here so he'd have an alibi for Katz's death. He could say we were with him when the chandelier fell. But before that he did have plenty of time to rig the electrical box."

"Paula West also doesn't have anyone to back her story. She could have given Cathy the night off so she could arrange the accident. She certainly has the electrical knowledge," Frank said.

His father shook his head. "I say we sleep on it," he said. "There's nothing more any of us can do tonight."

The next morning Joe and Frank helped themselves to a big catered breakfast. There were scrambled eggs, bacon, sausage, cinnamon rolls, orange juice, and coffee for the cast and crew.

"Man," Joe said. "You've got to admit—slasher movie crews sure do eat good."

"Yeah," Frank agreed. "And now that we've been fed, let's get to work."

"And, I say we start by questioning Paula again. Wasn't it strange that she was so quick to arrive on the scene yesterday?"

"We can try to question her, but for some reason, I don't think we're her two favorite people," Frank said.

"Maybe we went about it wrong last time. Remember what Aunt Gertrude always says?

You can catch more flies with honey than with vinegar," Joe said.

"Observe," he continued, walking up to Paula's door and rapping on it with his knuckles.

Paula opened the door. "What do you want?" she said to Joe in an unfriendly tone.

"We wanted to apologize for upsetting you the other day, Miss West," Joe said. "We in no way meant to imply that you were involved with Andrew Warmouth's murder."

Paula softened, smiling and opening the door wider. "Oh, it wasn't anything you said. I've just been under a lot of pressure lately. I'm the one who should apologize."

Paula took a step back. "Come on in, guys. I've got a pitcher of iced tea inside."

Joe and Frank exchanged a satisfied smile and walked into Paula's trailer. They sat at a small wooden table as Paula poured them each a glass of iced tea. Though it was only nine o'clock in the morning, the day was already extremely warm. Joe knew that a glass of cold tea would really hit the spot.

Joe and Frank talked for a while with Paula, but the discussion remained limited to Paula's profession.

"Want to see some of my work?" she asked.

The Hardys both nodded. Paula disappeared into the back room, and when she reemerged a few seconds later she was carrying a rubber arm that was wired to a remote-control box. Joe knew the arm was fake, but he was amazed at how real it looked. There was even hair on the forearm. Paula laid the arm on the table, and Joe could see what looked like veins running through the arm's wrist. She had thought of every detail.

"This is what made me famous," Paula bragged. "Nobody does body parts better than Paula West!"

Paula operated the remote box, and the arm began to move. The hand rose, pointing a finger at Frank. The hand made a peace sign. The hand snapped its fingers.

"That's incredible," Frank muttered.

Joe and Frank watched the hand for a few minutes, then Frank reminded Joe of the time. Joe remembered that they wanted to go to the Beaufort Hotel to question Harold and Kitty Hughes.

Outside Paula's trailer, Joe and Frank were interrupted by someone calling to them.

"There you are," the voice said. "I've been looking all over for you two."

Joe turned to find Shane Katz directly behind him.

"What can we do for you?" Frank asked.

"I talked to Gold, and he wants things to proceed as usual. Paula seems to think she can finish the film without the items the sheriff has confiscated. We're doing a zombie scene late this afternoon, and though I'm still quite leery of Matthew, the sheriff promised me he'd be at the shooting,'' Katz said.

''We'll be back before the shoot,'' Joe said. ''Could you tell us how to get to the Beaufort Hotel?'' Joe asked Katz.

''Sure.'' Katz gave them directions. The hotel was only seven miles south on the main thruway.

Joe and Frank thanked Katz, then walked to their rented car. They drove down the small country freeway, which cut through the heart of forest. ''Great scenery,'' Joe remarked. ''I hope we get a chance to explore it before we go home.''

''Depends on how fast we solve this case, brother,'' Frank said, pulling the car onto the small gravel driveway beside the Beaufort Hotel.

They entered the lobby of the building and approached a thin man who sat behind the front desk with his feet propped up on the counter. Joe waited several seconds for the man to look up from the dog-eared paperback he was reading.

''Excuse me,'' Joe said to the man. ''Could you tell us which room Harold and Kitty Hughes are in?''

''Number thirteen,'' the man replied, not looking up from his book. ''Take the hallway to your left and look on the right-hand side. Stop when you see the door with a one and a three on it.''

''Thanks,'' Joe grumbled.

As they made their way to the room, Joe suddenly chuckled.

"What's so funny?" Frank asked.

"Don't you find it hard to believe that a superstitious man like Harold Hughes would stay in a room numbered thirteen?" Joe replied.

"I guess so," Frank said.

Frank knocked lightly on the door. An elderly blue-haired woman wearing a pink smock answered the door.

"Yes?" she said pleasantly.

"Mrs. Hughes?" Frank asked.

"That's right," the woman replied.

"Good morning, ma'am," Frank continued. "I'm Frank Hardy. This is my brother, Joe. We've been asked by Fourteen Karat Movie Studios to investigate the murder of Andrew Warmouth. Would you mind if we asked you a few questions?"

"Oh, dear me," Kitty Hughes said, opening the door. "Come right in. I'm afraid that you can stay only for a moment. My husband, Harold, is out, and I have a few errands to run myself."

"We'll try to make it fast," Joe reassured her.

"Do you have any idea who might want to murder Andrew Warmouth? You knew him, didn't you?" Frank asked.

"Yes, I did," Mrs. Hughes said. She took a deep breath. "It was the spirits in the house," she said solemnly. "And if you boys know what's good for you, you'll stay away from there, too."

"Thank you, Mrs. Hughes," Joe said, exasperated. He had hoped that the woman would be more rational than her husband had been. But clearly the two were exactly alike.

The Hardys asked a few more questions, then began to leave. "Just a minute," Mrs. Hughes said. She thrust a box of brownies into Joe's hands. "Give these to that sweet boy, Matthew, who visits me."

Joe couldn't believe his ears. "Matthew Clervi—the Reaper?"

"Yes, that's right, Matthew. He's a doll. He's nothing like that character he plays. In fact, he told me he doesn't want to play the Reaper anymore and would do anything to get out of his contract," Mrs. Hughes said.

Stunned, Joe and Frank said goodbye to Mrs. Hughes, returned to their car, and headed back to the set. Joe sat on the passenger side while Frank drove. As they cruised back down the country road, Joe noticed that the branches of the trees on either side met over the road and formed a tunnel. It was dark and quiet and a little unsettling.

The blanketed silence was disrupted in a minute by the unmistakable sound of a gunshot.

"Where did that come from?" Frank said, alarmed. "Do you think someone's hunting?"

"I don't know," Joe said. "I can't think what

would be in season now. I can't make out anyone through the trees, either."

Another shot rang out, and this time Joe heard up close the metal ping it made when it struck. Their rear bumper had taken the full impact. "Why are they shooting at us?" he asked his brother.

"Not us," Frank answered. "Someone's aiming at our gas tank!"

Chapter 9

"STOP THE CAR!" Joe shouted.

Frank hit the brakes, and Joe pushed open the door and rolled out as the third shot found its target. The gas tank exploded with a deafening roar. A ball of flame separated Joe from the car. He rolled farther from the inferno.

Joe looked but could not see Frank. "Frank?" Joe whispered at first, panic quickly spreading through him. "Frank!" Joe exclaimed, arching up and scuttling crablike back to the car.

No, Joe thought, his head swimming with dread. Please, no.

He let out an audible sigh of relief as he saw his brother crawl into a drainage ditch several feet from the flaming car. He followed Frank's example and tumbled into the muddy ditch, sliding up close to his brother.

"Boy, am I glad to see you," Joe said.

"Me, too. But stay down!" Frank commanded. "You might get your head blown off!"

Joe and Frank waited several moments. Joe listened to the car burn, his mind flashing back to a day at the Bayport mall when his car had blown up, taking his girlfriend, Iola, with it. Joe pushed down the memory, wondering how long it would be before he'd begin to forget.

Finally he lifted his head and peered out of the ditch. Joe could see nothing but the trees.

"We should look for shells," Joe said, climbing out of the ditch. He needed to do something—take some sort of action.

"Where do we start?" Frank asked, climbing out of the ditch. "This road cuts right through the woods. Whoever shot at us could have been perched in any one of hundreds of trees. We don't even know what side the sniper was on when he fired. And we don't know if whoever did this is still around."

As if in answer to Frank's question, Joe heard a car engine rumble to life. Tires squealed, and the sound of a speeding vehicle filled the air.

"There must be a path farther back in the woods," Frank said.

"Let's check it out," Joe said.

"What about the car?" Frank turned toward the vehicle that was still burning in the middle of the road.

"I don't think we have to worry about anyone

stealing it," Joe said. "Come on. We'll find a phone and call the fire department. The fire seems to be contained."

Joe and Frank worked their way through the heavy brush. They walked a quarter of a mile through the dense foliage before they discovered a small dirt road leading to another road that ran parallel to the one they'd been traveling on. Both roads were deserted.

The gunman was long gone. Joe looked for spent shells on the way back to what was left of the rented car. He found nothing.

"Well," Frank said, "do you have any guesses?"

"I don't know who could have been waiting to ambush us," Joe said. "But Mrs. Hughes did say Harold was gone. He could have been somewhere near the hotel. He might have seen us and then come here, knowing which way we would head to go back to Horror House."

"Whoever fired on us would have to have been able to climb one of these trees. I think the bottom growth is too thick to shoot through from this distance," Frank said. "Harold looks like he's in his late sixties. Could he have climbed up a tree and back down in the time the gunman did?"

"I don't know," Joe said. "I also don't know what motive Harold would have for killing Warmouth, but I do know that the two of us dying in a car explosion while investigating the murder would fit in with Harold's curse nonsense."

"We'd better walk back into town and call the fire department," Frank said.

Joe and Frank started to head back to the main road. "Now we know that someone is definitely out to get us," Joe said. "The only person who knew we were going to the hotel was Katz. Could he have told someone on the set where we were?"

"He's scared of Clervi," Frank said. "I can't picture him casually mentioning where we were to Matt."

"How about Paula West?" Joe asked.

"She's a possibility," Frank replied. "He had to have told her about the zombie scene this afternoon. He may have mentioned that we'd left for a while but would be back in time for makeup."

Joe and Frank were back at the car now. The flames were dwindling, and the fire still hadn't spread to the bush. "After we call the fire department, let's try to examine that shot in the bumper," Joe suggested.

"Okay," Frank replied, setting a fast pace back toward Beaufort. "Let's examine our suspects again, too. There's Matthew Clervi. Though both of us thought he was being set up, we have to remember the chandelier accident and how badly Clervi wants out of his role. And Paula West. Because of her expertise and her dislike of Warmouth, she could have easily engineered the accidents."

"But Katz vouched for her for the acid incident," Joe reminded his brother.

"True," Frank said. "But Paula herself compared her job to that of a magician's. And you know what they say about the hand being quicker than the eye. She might have managed to slip the acid into the flask even with Katz present."

"Cathleen Bowley has to be a suspect, too," Joe said, "but we haven't been able to turn up either a motive or evidence on her."

"And our final suspects are Harold and Kitty Hughes," Frank said. "Are the Hugheses engineering these accidents, trying to stop production because they aren't happy with the films?"

"There's one more suspect," Joe added.

"Who?" Frank asked.

"The house," Joe replied half-seriously. "What if evil spirits really are trying to halt the production?"

"Have you ever heard of a ghost firing a shotgun or driving a car?" Frank asked sarcastically. "Come on, Joe. I've been telling you since we were little kids. There are no such things as ghosts."

"Who was the one who believed in Santa Claus until he was twelve years old?" Joe teased.

"Come on," Frank said. "Let's pick up the pace and find a phone."

* * *

Joe hung up the pay phone receiver. "The fire department is on its way," he said, stepping out of the booth in front of the Beaufort Hotel.

Joe looked around the rustic town of Beaufort. Downtown was made up of only four or five buildings: a post office, a general store, a hotel, and the sheriff's office. Where the fire station was Joe didn't know.

Joe studied his reflection in the glass booth. His clothes and face were filthy from the dive he had taken in the drainage ditch. He tried to straighten his gritty hair by running a hand back through it.

Frank, who looked just about the same as Joe, dug into his pants pocket and pulled out some change. "Here," he said, handing it to Joe. "Call Dad and ask him to come pick us up. I'm going over to the general store to buy us a couple of sodas."

Joe dialed the security phone. A guard answered and informed Joe that Fenton had been called away on an emergency. He told Joe that Fenton had left a letter for them and a message to carry on with the investigation.

"That's all he said?" Joe asked the security guard.

"He was in a rush," the man replied. "But he did say he'd call as soon as he could to explain everything. Oops, sorry, got to go—I was just beeped."

Joe hung up the phone and stepped back out of the booth. Frank was back, toting two bottles of root beer. "Is Dad on his way?" Frank asked.

"No," Joe said, and explained what the guard had told him.

Frank nodded, surprised. "So we're on our own."

"And we're also seven miles from the house," Joe said. "Should we call for a ride?"

"Well, you wanted to explore the country-side," Frank reminded him. "We could make it on foot."

Once again Joe and Frank found themselves walking along the country road. They walked a couple of miles before they saw the fire truck in the distance. Two fire fighters were shoveling dirt from the side of the road onto the car, which was now a blackened husk. Joe walked as close to the car as the fire fighters allowed. He noticed several holes in the car above the bumper.

"Whoever shot at us was definitely using a shotgun," Joe said.

"Then it's easy," Frank said. "We find out who had a license to possess a rifle on the set."

"You're thinking of New York law," Joe said. "We're in Texas. You don't need a license or permit to own a rifle."

Joe heard a siren nearing them. Sheriff Thornall's patrol car was approaching from the direction of Horror House. Thornall parked his car on the side of the road, got out, and sauntered up to Joe and Frank.

"Well, what have we here?" Thornall said, staring at the car. "I'd hate to see the insurance premiums you kids pay."

"Sheriff," Frank said, "someone shot at our car."

"I can see that," Thornall said. "You boys have to be careful. We get a few rambunctious hunters who like to shoot deer out of season in this area. It's happened before. Somebody's shot at your car by mistake."

"You don't really think this was an accident," Joe said incredulously. "Whoever did this took off without an apology."

"The guy was probably scared," Thornall said. "If it was someone out to get you, I think he would have finished the job."

"I think that someone wants us out of the way for investigating Warmouth's murder," Joe insisted, growing angry with the sheriff. "Warmouth's murderer is trying to kill us."

"That's not possible," Thornall said, shaking his head.

"Why not?" Frank asked.

"No murderer is going to get you, because I've had the murderer in custody for over an hour now," Thornall said smugly. "Matthew Clervi—the Reaper!"

Chapter 10

FRANK WAS STUNNED by Thornall's announcement. "What evidence did you use to arrest him?" he asked.

"I don't have to tell you boys anything, but maybe you'll learn something if I do," Thornall drawled. "I knew it was Clervi all along. The murder weapon was a scythe, and Clervi was the Reaper. Simple. I finally got a search warrant from Judge Parker. When I searched Clervi's trailer this morning, I found several electrical tools in a shoe box under his bed. I also found a wire stripper and a pair of wire clippers—the same kind of tools someone would need to rig a chandelier."

"If someone was trying to frame Clervi, though, they might have planted the tools in the trailer," Joe said.

"Why are you kids trying to prove he's innocent? I caught him with the goods in his trailer," Thornall said.

"If Clervi did rig the chandelier, why would he keep incriminating evidence under his bed? Surely he had to realize that eventually you'd get a search warrant," Frank said.

"Yeah, if it were me, I'd get rid of the tools. I can't imagine anyone who'd be stupid enough to keep them," Joe added.

"No one ever accused Matthew Clervi of being a genius," Thornall said, his eyes narrowing. "The way you boys are talking, I'd almost swear you were in cahoots with that nut."

"We have alibis for every incident," Frank said simply, not challenging the sheriff.

"I'm sure you do," Thornall grunted. "Get in the squad car. I'm taking you fellas back to the set."

Frank and Joe got in the back of Thornall's squad car. The ride back to the movie set was a quiet one, the silence interrupted only by an occasional buzz on the police band. Frank wasn't sure what to think of Clervi. So much evidence pointed to him, but something didn't fit. He couldn't put his finger on what was troubling him, but he also knew he and Joe didn't have all the facts on this case.

Thornall pulled up to the security gate and was quickly let in by the guard. Frank gazed out at the crowd of fans lining the fence. They were all young, some dressed as the Reaper in handmade robes and hoods.

"Punk idiots," Thornall muttered.

The sheriff pulled into the parking lot and stopped the car. Frank reached for the door handle. He groped the door panel for a few seconds before he remembered that police cars have no handles on the inside to prevent prisoners from escaping. Thornall got out of the car and opened the door for Frank and Joe.

"See you boys later," Thornall said, climbing back into the driver's seat. "I've got a prisoner to question." Thornall backed out of the driveway and pulled away.

Frank and Joe started back to their trailer when Joe suddenly stopped. "Frank, aren't all visitors to the set logged in at the gate?"

"Yeah," Frank said, understanding immediately. "Let's see who showed up on the night of Warmouth's murder."

Frank and Joe strode over to the security booth. Eddie, the guard, was inside drinking a cup of coffee and reading a newspaper.

"How's it going, Eddie?" Frank asked.

Eddie raised his eyes from his newspaper and smiled. "Pretty good, Frank. I've just been keeping an eye on that mob outside the fence," he said, motioning through the booth window at the fans who were peering over to see if the Hardys were anybody famous.

"Could we see the log book, Eddie?" Joe asked. "It's for our investigation."

The guard hesitated a second, then shrugged. "Sure." He handed Frank the leather-bound tablet.

Frank opened the book and turned to the date of Warmouth's murder. He scanned down the page. "There were only two visitors that night. They came during dinner break. Harold and Kitty Hughes, and a Robert Rinaldi."

"What time did they leave?" Joe asked.

"I can't tell," Frank said. "This log book looks like someone spilled something on it. The departure column is all smeared."

"Yeah," Eddie said to Frank. "Smitty, the guard on duty that night, spilled his coffee."

"Where can we find Smitty?" Joe asked.

"He's out sick with a bad stomach virus," Eddie replied. "Besides, if you want him to tell you about that night, the guy's hopeless. He has a real short-term memory," Eddie joked. "He probably doesn't remember what happened yesterday."

Frank and Joe handed the log back to Eddie, thanked him, and took off for their trailer, anxious to clean the grime from their bodies.

On the way they ran into Mike Sinnochi. "Man," Mike said, staring at the Hardys' clothes. "What happened to you?"

"It's a long story," Joe said.

"Can we ask you something, Mike?" Frank asked.

"Sure," Mike replied.

"Do you know a Robert Rinaldi?"

"Yeah, sure," Mike said.

"He was here the night of the murder. Do you know anything about his visit?" Joe asked.

"He showed up during dinner break to see Warmouth. He's the head of Excalibur Pictures, the company responsible for the *Midnight Massacre* horror film series. Why?"

"We saw his name on the security log," Frank explained. He was excited. A visit from a rival producer might be the missing piece of the puzzle that he was searching for.

"Yeah, he and Warmouth talked in private in Warmouth's trailer," Mike went on. "It ended in an argument, though. I heard them screaming at each other and saw Rinaldi storm out of the trailer."

"Why didn't you mention this before?" Frank asked.

Mike shrugged. "Every time Warmouth and Rinaldi got together, they ended up in a shouting match. The two movie series are similar and the scripts are closely guarded by both studios. Rinaldi has insisted for a couple of years that Warmouth was smuggling *Midnight Massacre* scripts out of the Excalibur office and using the outlines for *Horror House*."

"Do you think Warmouth was stealing scripts?" Joe asked.

"Hey, man, *Horror House* does ten times better than *Midnight Massacre* at the box office," Mike said, laughing. "I always figured Rinaldi was just jealous."

"Do you remember seeing Rinaldi leave?" Joe asked.

"No, I saw him leave Warmouth's trailer, but I didn't actually see him leave the set. But, hey, I was working so hard I wouldn't have noticed a bomb drop on the set," Mike said.

"Well, thanks for telling us about it," Frank said.

"I hope it helps. I'm sorry I didn't mention it sooner. I've been so busy that I just didn't think twice about the whole thing," Mike said apologetically.

"It might have an effect on Matthew Clervi's arrest," Frank remarked.

"Yeah, we can't leave any stone unturned now," Joe added.

Mike looked shocked. "Matt was arrested?"

"Yeah," Joe said. "Didn't you hear about it?"

"I had to leave here for a while," Mike said. "I got back just about the same time Thornall dropped you guys off."

Joe filled Mike in on the details concerning Clervi's arrest.

Mike stared at the Hardys, dumbfounded. "I

can't believe they think Matt's responsible. He's not capable of murder."

"That's why your information came at just the right time," Frank said. "If Clervi is innocent, we still have time to prove it."

"I hope you guys can do it," Mike said. "Oh, listen, you have about two hours before the zombie scene. Matt's not in it, so I'm sure the filming will continue without him, if I know Leonard Gold."

"Thanks," Joe said.

The Hardys continued on to their trailer, where Frank flipped a quarter to see who would get the shower first.

"You win again, brother," Frank said.

After they finished cleaning up, Frank reminded Joe that they had to stop by the security trailer to get the letter their dad had left for them.

When they stepped outside their trailer, Frank found a note taped to the front door. It read: Call Gold. Urgent! They must not have heard anyone knocking because of the shower running.

Frank stepped back inside immediately. He picked up the cellular phone on the nightstand and dialed Gold's number. Gold's secretary immediately put her boss on the line.

"This business of arresting Matthew is a disaster!" Gold exclaimed before Frank could even say hello. "I insist that you stay on and try to clear him. If he goes to prison, Fourteen Karat Studios will go down the tubes!"

"Excuse me for asking," Frank said, "but how would Clervi's no longer being in the film affect the series? After all, you can't see his real face. Who'd even know who's under all that makeup."

"Matthew has been on talk shows and has his picture taken without his makeup for magazine interviews. The fans love him. He gets thousands of letters a week," Gold roared.

"We'll do our best," Frank reassured Gold. He hung up the phone and relayed the conversation to Joe.

"He expects us to clear Clervi before the publicity puts Fourteen Karat Studios under?" Joe asked incredulously.

Frank nodded. "That's what Gold wants to prevent. Personally, I'm more interested in keeping an innocent man from being sent to prison," Frank said. He didn't think much of Gold and his attitude toward his workers—as though they were money-making machines instead of human beings.

"Before we do anything else, we've got to pick up Dad's letter," Joe told Frank.

"We're too pressed for time," Frank disagreed. "We have to get into makeup if we want to make the shoot."

Frank and Joe hurried toward the special-effects trailer, where Cathy Bowley prepared them for the scene in record time. Forgetting about their father's note, they left the trailer. Once outside Frank realized they had twenty minutes until they were called.

"Great," said Joe. "Let's go see Shane Katz. I have a couple of questions I want to ask him."

As Joe and Frank approached Katz's trailer, they were surprised to find its front door open. Katz was standing in the living room, his back to them, shouting into a telephone.

"Now that I have the say-so over this project, the next film will be quite different!" he ranted. "The *Horror House* series will finally be done the way it should have been from the start! I expect the papers from Andy's lawyer any day now."

Katz turned around and saw the Hardys. "I'll call you back," he said abruptly into the phone and hung up.

"So," Katz said, smiling uncomfortably, "how long have you guys been standing there?"

"Just a few seconds," Frank said.

"Isn't your detective work done?" Katz demanded. "Clervi's in jail."

"Gold wants us to stay on," Joe said. "We were brought in to help my dad with security, anyway. We're here to the end."

"I see," Katz said. "All right. Well, today in your scene you zombie slaves have to burst out of the Horror House storm cellar. It's the place where the Reaper buries his victims. Then you'll converge on the heroine, who'll be standing on the front porch of the house. You might want to go through it once before we start."

Frank and Joe walked back to the house in silence. As they approached the storm cellar on the side of the house, Frank finally said, "I wonder who Katz was talking to? And I wonder what kind of papers he'll be getting from Warmouth's lawyer?"

"We'll check it out tonight," Joe assured him.

"It doesn't look like the equipment has been set up for the zombie scene yet," Frank said. "We're the only ones here."

"Maybe everything's inside." Joe gingerly lifted the double doors to the cellar.

Frank shivered as they walked down the cellar steps into cold blackness. Frank started to turn around to leave, but just then the doors were slammed shut. Frank heard a metal bar being slid through the door handles. They were trapped!

"Hold on," Joe said. "I've got my penlight."

Joe turned the light on and shined it down around their feet. The cellar floor was crawling with scorpions—and they were all crawling straight for Frank and Joe!

Chapter 11

"UH, FRANK," Joe said, backing up the stairway as the scorpions came closer. "Are Texas scorpions poisonous?"

"I don't think one sting from a scorpion is dangerous, but I don't know how serious several stings would be," Frank replied, inching toward the door. "And I don't want to find out."

Frank turned and rushed up the steps to the bulkhead door, lifting his back against it.

Joe added his weight. Together the Hardys lifted their shoulders against the door. "We're trapped down here!" Joe shouted at the top of his lungs. "Somebody open the door!" No one came.

Joe turned and shone his penlight across the basement floor. The scorpions were crawling up the stairs now. He shuddered at the thought of fighting them off. A few feet from the stairs he spotted a rusty crowbar lying in the dirt. Scorpions were crawling all over the tool. Joe took a deep breath, leapt off the steps, and reached for the tool, brushing the scorpions off quickly. He rushed back up the stairs.

"Okay. Now try," Joe said, prying up on the door far enough for Frank to slip his hand through and remove the metal bar.

The doors opened, and Joe found himself looking into the worried face of Cathy Bowley.

"What happened? I heard someone yell and came running," she said as Joe and Frank slammed the doors shut behind them.

"There's a whole nest of scorpions down there," Joe said, searching himself to make sure none were clinging to his clothes.

Katz walked up to the Hardys as the crew was gathering around, asking what had happened. "What's going on?" Katz demanded louder than the others.

Frank relayed the details.

"Okay," Katz said. "Everybody stay calm. Scorpions like cool places to get away from the heat. I'll have someone call an exterminator to clean the cellar tomorrow. Let's knock off for the rest of the night. The tension has been terrible, and we've all earned a break. We'll have to pull some overtime next week to meet the schedule, but who cares?"

The crew dispersed. "I'm convinced that someone is out to get us," Frank said, remembering Fenton's letter to them in the security trailer and heading off to retrieve it.

"Could it be Katz?" Frank asked. "He did suggest that we go over to the cellar. And what about that phone call we overheard?"

"You can't hang Katz for saying he wants to do a better job with the series than Warmouth did," Joe said. "With Warmouth's death, I guess Katz has complete control over the project now. But those papers he said he would receive from Warmouth's lawyer—I wonder if Katz inherited something from Andrew Warmouth?"

"It's possible," Frank replied.

When Joe and Frank received Fenton's letter, Joe opened it and read it to Frank:

> "Dear Frank and Joe,
>
> Something big is brewing in Los Angeles. An old friend with the FBI called and asked me to help him on a case. It's urgent. National security may be threatened if I don't act now. Continue with the investigation. I'll call once things settle down. Take care,
>
> Dad"

"At least one of us gets to spend the summer near the beach," Frank said. "I just hope he's okay."

"Dad's always been able to take care of himself," said Joe as he refolded the note. "Let's get this makeup off our faces. Then let's find out where Paula West was today."

Joe knocked on the front door of the special-effects trailer. Cathy Bowley opened the door, smiling brightly at Joe and Frank. "Hi, guys," she said. "What can I do for you?"

"Could we ask you a few questions?" Frank asked.

"Sure," Cathy said, stepping outside. "Can we talk out here? I just got through mixing some chemicals. The trailer's pretty thick with fumes."

"We can talk right here," Joe said.

"Do you know where Paula West went today?" Frank asked.

"No. She said she was taking the day off and told me to take care of everything," Cathy said. "I don't know where she went."

"Paula told us that she didn't think you were ready to do the special makeups the other day," Joe said. "And yet, today, you applied our makeup. Do you know why?"

"I've been practicing," Cathy bragged. "Paula decided the only way to learn was by getting my feet wet. Besides, the regular makeup people were here, and Mike was around to give me a hand if there were any problems."

"Thanks, Cathy," Frank said.

"I was just going to lock up the trailer and go

into town for dinner. I have to get away. You guys want to join me?" Cathy asked, pulling the front door shut and locking it.

"Sure," Joe said eagerly. He was hungry and the prospect of spending an hour or so with Cathy Bowley was an added attraction.

"I guess we could use a bite to eat," Frank agreed.

Cathy walked down the steps and paused to slip the key under the stair tread. Joe glanced at Frank and hoped his brother was thinking the same thing he was.

It was dark when Cathy dropped Joe and Frank off after dinner at the security gate.

"Thanks for picking up the tab," she said to Joe as the Hardys climbed out of the car.

"No problem," Joe said, shutting the car door. "Any time."

"Are you sure you won't join me for a movie in Fort Worth?" Cathy asked. "There are a lot of good flicks playing."

"It's tempting," Frank said. "But we've got work to do."

Cathy nodded, then backed the car out of the driveway.

The security gate was lifted, and Frank and Joe stepped onto the property. They were going to head straight to their trailer when Eddie yelled to them, wide-eyed, "Someone's on the property! And he's dressed like the Reaper!"

"How did he get in?" Joe asked, glancing

around at the fence that shut in the Hughes property.

"I don't know. He didn't get by here, I promise. I just got a call from one of the crew who spotted him. He's carrying a scythe. The guy who saw him couldn't tell whether it was fake or not," Eddie replied.

"Okay, Eddie. You check by the trailers. Joe and I'll check the house," Frank ordered. "Be careful. This guy might be the killer."

Eddie unstrapped his gun. "Don't worry about me," he said, turning and running toward the trailers. "I'm a professional."

"Come on," Frank said to Joe, sprinting to the house.

Joe reached the front door before Frank. The house was shut down and the grounds were deserted. The crew was either in their trailers or off the set, Joe realized.

Joe noticed that the front door, usually locked after filming, was open slightly. He took out his penlight and examined the doorframe.

"Looks like someone forced it," Frank muttered over Joe's shoulder.

"Let's do it," Joe said, easing the door open.

Joe stepped into the hallway. The house was dark. He reached for a light switch, then realized that he and Frank might have the advantage if the house stayed dark. Joe turned on his penlight and scanned the living room, den, and dining room.

Joe shone the light on the stairway, and followed the spot of light up the steps to the second floor. The light fell on a figure dressed as the Reaper.

"There he is!" Joe shouted.

The figure moved to the left and disappeared in the darkness. Joe switched on the living room light so he and Frank could see to mount the stairs.

Joe reached the top first and headed for the doors on the left. The first door opened to a bathroom. The second revealed a bedroom. Before Joe could open the third door, it burst open, knocking him backward into Frank. Joe and Frank both fell to the floor as the robed figure ran back down the stairway.

"Get him!" Joe shouted. Picturing how badly he was going to clobber this guy for knocking him down, Joe raced down the stairway and chased the intruder out of the house. The intruder stopped by a trash can stationed at the end of the parking lot.

Joe sped up. "That's right, bozo," he muttered through gritted teeth. "Hold that pose." Joe ducked down, ready to spring and tackle the dark figure. Joe's eyes widened as the fugitive knocked the can over, and rolled it directly toward Joe.

Joe's legs hit the aluminum trash can, causing him to flip over and land flat. All the wind was knocked out of him. As Joe looked up, he saw Frank sail overhead.

Joe arched up just in time to see Frank hit the intruder with a flying tackle and bring him to the ground.

Grateful and more than a little relieved, Joe rubbed his battered limbs and hoisted himself painfully to his feet. Maybe Frank has a point about me always losing my head, Joe thought as he walked over to where Frank had pinned the struggling figure to the ground. Nothing was broken, but he was pretty sure that he'd ache for a few days.

"Who do we have here?" Joe asked flippantly, bending down and pulling an imitation Reaper mask off the intruder. He shone his penlight into the intruder's face.

The answer to his question came as quite a shock. He was only a kid! The young man's face was marked with acne, and silver braces glinted from his half-open mouth. The kid's eyes were squeezed shut with fear.

"Turn the light off, please," the young man whined.

"What do you think you're doing?" Frank asked, letting the kid up.

"I just wanted to get a souvenir prop," the kid insisted. "I figured if I dressed up like the Reaper, no one would recognize me."

He doesn't know Clervi's in jail, Joe realized.

Frank hauled the youth to his feet. The kid

looked around, frantically. "My scythe, man. Where's my scythe?"

Joe scanned the ground with his penlight, illuminating the plastic toy that Frank had crushed when he tackled the youth.

Amused and angry, the Hardys escorted the young man off the set, then found Eddie and explained everything to him.

"Boy, I wish Dad had been around to see that," said Frank. "Oh, well. The fun's over. I say we go back to our trailer, wait until midnight, then use the key Cathy hid under the step to search the trailer." Frank started to walk away from the guard booth.

"Let's also hope that Paula West doesn't decide to work tonight," Joe said, hurrying to keep up with him.

Joe and Frank went back to their trailer and cleaned up, passing the time talking.

"I think we have to pay a visit to Excalibur Pictures and talk to Robert Rinaldi," Joe said, stretching out on Frank's bed, which was pulled down. "I'm curious to know what he and Warmouth talked about."

"Let's do that tomorrow," Frank agreed. "Now, get your shoes off my bed. They're dirty."

When midnight finally arrived, the brothers stole quietly toward Paula's work trailer. No one was out moving around, and Joe was positive they had made it unnoticed to the trailer. He retrieved the key from under the step.

"Hope we can find evidence that'll prove Clervi's innocent," Joe whispered, unlocking the door and silently inching it open. "I bet Thornall didn't search very hard for clues because he's so convinced that Clervi's guilty." Joe turned on his penlight once they were inside.

He shone the light around the room, spotting the many boxes that Paula West had lined up against the walls. "This room is so full of stuff," Joe muttered, "that I don't even know where to begin."

"Try flashing that light around. Maybe something will jump out at us," Frank said.

"I hope you don't mean that literally," Joe replied, shining the penlight on Paula's worktable.

Frank started to answer, but the words caught in his throat.

The light revealed the cold, dead face of Andrew Warmouth!

Chapter 12

FRANK STARED at the head in speechless horror. That was all there was, a head. Warmouth's eyes were open, and his mouth was locked in an eternal scream.

Frank saw Joe reach out to touch the head.

Frank grabbed Joe's arm. "What are you doing?"

Joe gently pried Frank's fingers from his arm. "Relax," Joe said, reaching out once again to touch Warmouth's cheek. Frank watched in shocked silence.

Suddenly Joe laughed. "It's fake," he said.

Frank released the breath he had been holding. "It nearly scared me to death," he admitted.

"Yeah, but what scares me is, why would Paula West create a head of Warmouth?" Joe asked.

"That's a good question," Frank replied, surveying the other items on the table.

Frank shook his head as he surveyed the morbid assortment of fake body parts on the table. He sifted through noses, ears, fingers, and toes. He picked up a knife and pressed the blade against the palm of his hand. It didn't retract.

"I think it's a bleeder," Joe suggested, taking the knife from Frank's hand.

"What's a bleeder?" Frank asked, wondering if he really wanted to know. Some of this special-effects stuff could be really gross.

"Here," Joe said, pulling Frank's arm over and shoving the penlight into Frank's other hand. "I'll show you."

Joe ran the knife over Frank's palm. A wet, crimson gash appeared on Frank's skin. Frank pulled his arm away, startled.

"It's okay," Joe reassured his brother, who was studying his hand for a wound. "This knife holds a packet of fake blood. There's a button on the handle that you push to force the fake blood out of tiny holes on the edge of the blade."

Frank wiped his hands on his jeans, then remembered how much the jeans had cost him. He hoped fake blood washed out.

"Hey, Frank," Joe said.

Frank stared at his brother, who was holding two fake eyes in front of his face.

"I only have eyes for you," Joe crooned, tossing the orbs to Frank.

"Get serious," Frank said, setting the eyes on the table. "We're here to search for clues. I'll buy you toys when we get back home."

"Have a heart," Joe said, handing Frank a fake one from the worktable. "Check this out," Joe added, sticking a wire in the bottom of the fake organ. Joe picked up a small, rubber palm pump and attached it to the airhose that was protruding from the heart. He squeezed the pump. The heart began to constrict, then expand.

"This would make a swell Valentine for Callie," Joe teased.

"You are seriously demented," Frank said, putting the heart on the table.

"It runs in the family," Joe joked.

"Joe," Frank said, spotting something. "Check this out."

Frank picked up a mold. The face looked like Shane Katz, with Katz's eyes and mouth closed. "She was making one of Katz as well," Frank said.

Joe ran his finger through the mold. "I feel some hard traces of the latex mix in there," Joe said. "She definitely made a head of Katz. I wonder where it is?"

Joe slowly flashed the penlight around the room, but neither boy could spot it.

Joe then held the light on the mold.

"What's up?" Frank asked.

"I don't know," Joe said. "There's something peculiar about this mold, but I can't figure out what it is."

"Maybe it'll come to you later," Frank said. "What I want to know is why Paula created these heads of Warmouth and Katz."

"Let's look in these drawers," Joe said, using his light to outline a small filing cabinet next to the table.

Frank opened the top drawer and found nothing incriminating inside. It was stuffed with receipts for various chemicals and mechanical devices. The second and third drawers were full of similar papers. In the bottom one Frank found a padlocked metal box.

He put it on the worktable, and Joe started to pick the lock without hesitating.

"I'm not sure we should do that, Joe," Frank said, concerned that Paula West would walk in. If she saw what Joe was doing, she could have them arrested.

"Let me remind you that we've nearly been killed three times in the last two days," Joe replied. "Thornall thinks he has the guilty party when we know otherwise. After all, how could Clervi have shot at the car? The police won't help us, so we have to help ourselves."

The lock sprung open, and Joe raised the lid to peer inside. He pulled out a letter and handed it to Frank. Frank unfolded the letter and read it in the dim light from Joe's penlight.

"It's from Andrew Warmouth," Frank said. "It says, 'Work for Horror House, or everyone will know that your claim to fame was a sham.' What does that mean?"

"I can guess what it means," Joe said. "Paula's claim to fame was the radio-controlled mechanical body parts. Maybe she stole the idea from someone else. If it weren't for those parts Paula designed, she'd still be a low-paid assistant."

"So, maybe Warmouth found out and was blackmailing Paula," Frank added. He hesitated. "Blackmail is a very good motive for murder."

"Yeah," Joe agreed. "And it's the only reason I know of that would explain why Paula worked for Warmouth for so little money."

"We also can't ignore Paula's absence during today's shoot," Frank said excitedly. "Joe, I'd say she's our number-one candidate. But why would she save that incriminating letter—well, I guess people do stranger things."

Frank stuffed the letter into his pocket, relocked the metal box, and returned it to the bottom drawer. Then he and Joe left the trailer, replacing the key.

As they hurried back toward their trailer, Frank grew more confident than ever that Clervi had indeed been framed. They would need more evidence, though, he decided, before he could turn the letter over to the authorities.

Frank was so caught up in the case that he

almost failed to notice that the light in their trailer was on. "Joe," he said, reaching for the door handle, "didn't you turn off the light before we left?"

"Yeah, I did." Joe's expression froze. He stared at his brother.

"Someone's in our trailer!" Frank shouted, bursting inside with Joe on his heels.

But this time no Reaper waited to attack them. Instead, Sheriff Thornall sat waiting on the edge of Frank's bed. "Hello, boys. Out awfully late, aren't you?" he said gruffly.

"What can we do for you?" Frank asked, clearly shaken by the lawman's surprise visit.

"I'm glad you asked." Thornall stood up, slapping his holstered gun with an air of superiority. "You see, while I was making my nightly rounds around Beaufort, someone sneaked into the jailhouse and clubbed my deputy on the back of the head. He was the only officer there, and he has a habit of dozing off behind his desk. He didn't see who knocked him out, but when he woke up, Clervi was gone."

"What has that got to do with us?" Joe demanded indignantly.

"Well, what do you think?" Thornall said, smiling like the Cheshire cat.

"Why are you coming to us now?" Joe continued. "You didn't want us in on the investigation, so what does Clervi's escaping from jail have to do with—"

Joe paused, and Frank realized that Joe had answered his own question.

A very bad feeling was washing over Frank.

"Plenty," Thornall said, stepping menacingly toward the Hardys. " 'Cause I think you boys busted Clervi out!"

Chapter 13

FRANK COULDN'T BELIEVE what he'd heard.

"What are you saying?" Joe exclaimed, his temper flaring.

"You heard me," Thornall said. "You boys were in on this with Clervi from the start, weren't you?"

"Wait a minute, Sheriff," Frank said calmly. "What time did the jailbreak take place?"

"About seven-thirty," Thornall replied.

"We were on our way back from having dinner with Cathy Bowley at that time," Frank said.

"You can prove that?" Thornall asked.

"We sure can," Joe said. "Cathy drove us back herself."

"Listen, Sheriff, we're on the same side,"

Frank said. "Why don't you have a seat and listen to what we've found out?"

Thornall hesitated. "Well," he said at last, "it's probably a waste of time, but it might be good for a few laughs." He sat back down on the bed.

Frank told Thornall about their suspicion of Paula West. He gave Thornall every reason he and Joe had for thinking her capable of the murder. Finally he showed the sheriff the incriminating letter from Warmouth to Paula West.

Thornall's features softened, and Frank thought he might actually have managed to get through to the sheriff.

"You boys did some good detecting," Thornall said, sounding impressed with them despite himself. "Nevertheless, I've got an escaped prisoner on my hands and only two men on my force, one of whom is in the hospital with a concussion."

"Why don't you let us question Paula tomorrow?" Joe said. "If we discover anything useful, we'll come straight to you. This way you can continue your search for Clervi while we question Paula."

"Okay," Thornall agreed. "But I want you boys to know that I intend to check your alibi tomorrow. And if I find out you've lied to me, I'll be on you like warts on a toad!"

With that, Thornall lumbered out of the small trailer.

Maybe Thornall wasn't all bad, Frank thought.

He sighed. But at that time of night, who could tell?

"Let's hit the sack," he said to Joe. "We've got a busy day ahead of us."

The next morning Frank and Joe ate a quick breakfast of doughnuts and orange juice, then headed straight for the special-effects trailer. Cathy Bowley was inside, finishing a latex mask.

"If you're looking for Paula, she never made it back last night," Cathy said.

"She was out all night?" Joe asked, concerned. "Do you think anything might have happened to her?"

"Oh, no," Cathy said. "She usually stays at a hotel overnight in Fort Worth on her day off, then drives back the next day. She doesn't like to drive at night."

"Do you have any idea when she might get in?" Frank asked.

"I don't know exactly," Cathy said. "She has a little extra time coming to her, and she may take it today since there's not much happening. The River Oaks Cinema is having a triple horror movie feature that starts at noon. Paula loves horror movies, so you might be able to find her there."

Cathy, who was standing at the worktable, moved Warmouth's head aside to make room for a new mold.

"Why did Paula make heads of Katz and Warmouth?" Frank asked, motioning to the head.

"She made them for a party last Halloween," Cathy said. "It was Shane's idea." She looked up at Frank, suddenly puzzled. "At least, I think that's what she said."

Frank and Joe thanked Cathy, then left.

"So, what's next?" Joe asked Frank, discouraged, as they stepped outside.

"There's Mike Sinnochi." Frank waved at Mike.

"All filming's been canceled for today," Mike announced before Frank or Joe could say anything. Mike looked disgusted and extremely irritable. "Shane was called off the set this morning."

"What's up?" Joe asked.

"I don't know." Mike frowned. "Shane just told me he had an emergency to attend to and that he'd be back this evening. I've never seen anything like it. There's no way we're going to meet the schedule at this rate."

The Hardys agreed to check in with Mike later, in case of any new developments. As they continued toward their trailer, Frank said, "I need to use the phone."

"Who are you going to call?" Joe asked.

"Excalibur Pictures. I want to try to make an appointment with Robert Rinaldi," Frank replied. "We might as well use our time constructively."

When Frank finally reached Rinaldi's secretary on the phone, he explained that he was part of Fourteen Karat Studios' security force working with the Beaufort sheriff's office, and that he wanted to talk to Rinaldi about the murder.

The secretary put Frank on hold for a moment, then told him Rinaldi would see him in one hour. She gave Frank the directions to the Dallas office. Frank wrote them down on a notepad and thanked her.

"We're in," Frank informed Joe, hanging up the phone and stuffing the directions in his pocket. "We'll take Dad's car."

Rinaldi's secretary sent the Hardys right in to speak to Robert Rinaldi.

He was a tanned, balding man who stood up from behind his large desk to shake their hands. "Gentlemen," he said, motioning graciously to two chairs positioned in front of his desk. "Please have a seat."

"I'm Frank Hardy, and this is my brother, Joe," Frank said, sitting down.

"So, the two of you are sibling sleuths. Now, that's a good premise for a film," Rinaldi said, chuckling.

"I guess it would be," Joe agreed.

Rinaldi eased back into his reclining chair and clasped his hands together behind his head. "How can I help you?"

"We understand you were with Warmouth the

night he was killed. We also understand that the two of you had a disagreement," Frank said.

"Ah," Rinaldi said, nodding his head knowingly. "So you want to know if our dispute led to my killing Warmouth. Let me assure you, I was on the far side of Fort Worth at the time of Warmouth's murder. Besides having my chauffeur as a witness, I can also call upon a female acquaintance who dined with me when I returned that night."

"I see," Frank said. He didn't have to see the dead-end sign to know where this was heading.

"What about your accusations that Warmouth was stealing *Midnight Massacre* scripts?" Joe asked Rinaldi.

Rinaldi leaned forward, gripping the desk. "Let me tell you about Andrew Warmouth, my friends. He was a despicable man. I have it from reliable sources that the only person making money from the *Horror House* movies was Warmouth. He bound everyone on the crew to long-term contracts and paid them scale fees, otherwise known as minimum wage. Warmouth made money from the box office, merchandising, and video sales. He cut everyone else out of the rights."

"How could he do that?" Joe asked.

"When the first film went into production, he offered Katz, West, and everyone involved what seemed like good salaries. They all signed the contracts without noticing the fine print that stated their pay would remain the same in case of any sequels. They all had to work on four more films at the same rate as they had six years earlier. The Hugheses were also victims of Warmouth's dirty tactics."

"What did he do to them?" Frank asked.

"They signed a contract that enabled Warmouth to rent the house for the films. He promised them ten thousand dollars to make the first movie there. He bought their rights from them outright, cheating them out of any royalties, and then he talked them into signing a contract with a similar clause to the one in the crew's contract. The Hugheses receive only ten thousand for each film. It's their only source of income other than social security. And they can't sell the house."

"How do you know all of this?" Frank asked.

"I have my sources," Rinaldi said with a smile. "There's a lot of espionage in this business. Warmouth had someone in this office who was sending him our scripts. We never found out who the guilty party was, but I don't have to worry about nonsense like that anymore. I received a very reassuring call from Shane Katz yesterday."

"What has Katz got to do with this?" Joe asked.

"It's Katz's ball game now," Rinaldi said. "All the rights reverted to him upon Warmouth's death. And believe me, Shane Katz deserves every penny."

"You mean Katz was treated the same way as the rest of the crew?" Joe asked. "I thought he created the Reaper."

"He did. But when he approached Warmouth with the script for the first film, Andrew was already an established producer, while Shane was just starting in the business," Rinaldi replied. "It happens every day. The only decent thing Andrew ever did was will the rights of the series to Shane."

"Thank you for your time, Mr. Rinaldi," Frank said, rising from his seat to shake the man's hand.

Frank and Joe left the office in silence and headed for the elevator. The moment they entered it, Frank turned to Joe and said, "Shane Katz had a lot to gain from Warmouth's death."

"Yeah, but Mike Sinnochi vouched for him during the time of the murder," Joe reminded him.

"I'll bet when we overheard Katz talking on the phone, he was talking to Rinaldi. I know Katz has an alibi, but he needs to be considered," Frank said as the elevator stopped and the doors slid open.

"Maybe. But I still have my money on Paula West," Joe grumbled. "And I say we go find her."

Just past the Fort Worth city limits, Frank

pulled over at a gas station and called information for the number of the River Oaks Cinema. After calling for directions to the theater, the brothers drove straight there. "Just in time," Frank said as he paid for two tickets to the triple feature. "The first film's already started."

It took a moment for Frank's eyes to adjust to the dark once they entered the auditorium. Once they did, though, he counted six people scattered among the seats. Glancing for a moment at the screen, he registered an image of a young girl being chased through a graveyard by a vampire.

"Oh, wow," Joe whispered into Frank's ear. "This is a Hammer film. Classic ultra-low-budget. I read an article about it in *Gore* magazine."

Frank was impressed by Joe's knowledge of horror movies, but he was also annoyed that Joe was now more interested in the movie than in finding Paula West. "We're not here to watch the movie, Joe," Frank muttered.

"I know that," Joe said defensively. "I just thought you might find the film's history interesting. If I enlighten you a bit on modern horror movies, maybe you'll appreciate them better."

"When it comes to horror movies, just leave me in the dark," Frank said, taking a few steps forward and glancing at the couple who were seated in the middle row of seats.

Frank and Joe continued their slow march forward, checking every face until they reached a figure seated in the front row, directly in front of the screen.

"Last chance," Frank whispered as he and Joe checked out the last person. It was Paula, all right, and she was totally absorbed in the movie. Frank and Joe quietly sat down next to her.

Before Frank could decide what to say to her, a gunshot pierced the air!

Chapter 14

THE HARDYS fell to the floor, dragging Paula with them. Frank heard another shot ring out, and glanced up in time to see a huge hole appear in the movie screen. Everyone in the theater was screaming. Frank heard footfalls echo at his right and saw a dark figure slip out the back exit of the theater.

"Come on," Frank said, gripping Joe's shoulder. "He's getting away!"

Frank and Joe rushed to the exit. Stepping cautiously outside, they saw they were in an empty alley. The shooter had escaped.

Frank glanced at the door handle. "Check this out, Joe," he said. The door had been pried open from the outside, and the lock was broken.

"It looks like our gunman got in for free," Frank said.

Back in the theater, the film had been stopped and the lights were turned on. Frank and Joe approached the small crowd of theater patrons who were huddled together, confused and frightened.

"Is everyone okay?" Frank asked.

The five people—a middle-aged couple, an elderly woman, and two teenagers—nodded meekly.

"Did anyone see anything?" Joe asked.

"Are you kidding?" the elderly woman spoke up. "It happened too fast, and it was too dark to make out anything. All I knew when that gun went off was that I was going to kiss the floor! I didn't come up for air until the lights came on."

"What about the rest of you?" Frank asked.

The others slowly shook their heads.

"I know the movie wasn't great, but I didn't think it was that bad," the elderly woman told Frank, pointing to the large hole in the screen.

Frank felt a touch on his shoulder and turned around to see Paula West. "What's going on?" Paula asked Frank, her face as pale as a ghost's. Frank could see that her hands were shaking.

"Let's go into the lobby and talk," Frank said.

"Come on, Joe," Frank called to his brother, who was examining the emergency exit again.

Frank led Joe and Paula to the lobby, where they all sat down on a wooden bench. "Paula," Frank began, "we know that Warmouth was blackmailing you. We were suspicious of you from the start and thought you might have committed the murder. You had the special-effects expertise to rig the accidents, and you also had a very bad attitude when we questioned you about Warmouth. After the acid incident we thought you might have managed to slip acid into the flask, even with Shane present."

"We also thought you substituted the real scythe for the fake one during the mailman scene," Joe added. "When we discovered that the chandelier in the Horror House dining room was rigged, we suspected you again. What cinched it for us was your disappearance from the set yesterday."

"Someone tried to ambush us on the road yesterday and shot our car up," Frank continued, watching Paula for a reaction. "You were unaccounted for, so we were pretty sure you were responsible."

"Of course, we don't think that anymore," Joe reassured Paula.

Paula broke down and began to sob. "These aren't tears of guilt for Warmouth's murder," she said. "They are tears of relief. Yes, I stole the components for those mechanical parts from my first boss. I also stole all his notes on them before he had a chance to get a patent. I've been haunted by guilt for a long time. Warmouth was blackmailing me. He was the biggest rat in the business. But I didn't kill him."

"We know that now," Joe said. "And we're sure Sheriff Thornall will believe it, too. You know we have to take you to him?"

Paula nodded meekly. "Yes. I don't care. It feels good finally to have this off my conscience."

The Hardys and Paula were ready to make their exit when the Fort Worth police showed up.

"Stay put," an officer said to the trio. "I'll have to ask you a few questions."

"Oh, please," Joe groaned as the officer stepped past them into the auditorium. "Not another Thornall. Why don't we just tell him that someone really hated the flick?"

"I don't like the idea of hanging around here any more than you do," snapped Frank, "but the police need to know exactly what went down."

"Oh, absolutely," Joe said with a wink. "I'll be very up-front with him when he returns. Watch me."

Just then the officer returned to the lobby, taking notes on a small pad as he approached the Hardys and Paula.

"Names, please?" the officer said.

"Yes," Joe said. "I'm Joe Hardy. This is my brother, Frank, and Paula West."

The officer jotted down the information, then looked at Joe. "Can you tell me what happened here?"

"Sure. You see, my brother and I are working with Fourteen Karat Studios and the Beaufort sheriff's office to find the killer of a famous movie producer. My brother and I came here to question our main suspect, Miss West, when the real killer burst in through the emergency exit and started shooting at us. It was too dark to identify him."

"What?" The officer squinted at Joe. "What kind of game are you playing, kid? This is serious business. You go play detective with your brother and girlfriend somewhere else. And when a police officer questions you in the future, I suggest that you not kid around."

"Yes, sir," Joe said.

Frank, Joe, and Paula headed quickly for the exit.

"Works like a charm every time," Frank muttered.

"Yes, sir, there's nothing like telling the truth."

"That wasn't what I meant, Joe," Frank said sternly, but even he was grinning.

When Frank and Joe escorted Paula into Thornall's police station, the sheriff was there, having a cup of coffee. His disheveled appearance and bloodshot eyes made Frank wonder if he'd been up all night. Seeing that the cell in the police station was empty, Frank assumed Thornall hadn't found Clervi.

The Hardys told Thornall about the shooting incident, and then Paula told Thornall her story. The sheriff took a moment to digest all the new information. Then he stood up.

"So Clervi must have been following you guys," Thornall concluded.

"We don't think the murderer is Clervi," Joe said.

"Well, if it isn't Clervi or Miss West here, then who can it be?" Thornall asked.

"We don't know yet," Frank admitted. "But we're going to find out."

"I'll have to keep Miss West here for a while. I have a few more questions to ask her," Thornall said.

"We'd better head back to the set and see what we can dig up," Frank said to Joe.

Silent and worried, the Hardys drove back to the Hughes house. They arrived in time for dinner. They ate by themselves outside the catering truck and mulled over their suspects.

"Clervi wanted out of his contract to pursue more dramatic roles," Frank said. "The Hugheses were being taken advantage of by Warmouth. There's a good chance Paula is innocent, since those shots at the theater were aimed at her as well as us. Even if she was helping someone and trying to throw us off, I doubt she would have agreed to be shot at in the dark. Besides, she had no idea we were going to show up at the theater, unless Cathy Bowley was a plant. But I think the killer has been following us all day. And if that's true, Cathy can't be the shooter because she was here all day. Clervi definitely wasn't the one who shot at us on the way back from the hotel. So, considering the recent developments, I guess Harold and Kitty deserve our undivided attention."

"Harold and Kitty have a strong motive, but I have to admit that I can't really believe they committed the murder," Joe said. He paused and stared thoughtfully at his empty plate. "I still feel like we're missing something."

The brothers left the table and headed back to the security trailer. There was no message from Fenton.

"Anything special going on?" Frank asked the guard on duty.

"Not really," the guard replied. "We had a few fans sneak into the storm cellar earlier, but that was about the only excitement for the day."

"I know you guys have been keeping your eyes open since the murder," Joe said to the guard. "Have any of you noticed anything unusual?"

"I haven't seen anything. I spend most of my time just keeping people off the set. I've been too busy to pay attention to much else," the guard replied.

"Well, if you do notice something, you know where to find us," Frank said.

"That I do," the guard replied.

Frank and Joe walked outside. It was dark,

and they were both very tired. They headed back to their trailer.

Frank hoped that the next day would be a better one for the investigation. He wished their dad would call. They could use some help. Wearily he entered the trailer and sprawled out on his bed. "Oh, man," he said, rubbing his brow. "Now that my head's hit the pillow, I'm going to be dead to the world."

Joe snapped his fingers. "That's it, Frank!" Joe exclaimed, standing up. "The night of Warmouth's murder, Mike Sinnochi went into Katz's trailer and said Katz looked dead to the world. Katz used the mechanical head to create an alibi! He put the head in his bed, making it look like he was asleep."

Frank sat up, his weariness forgotten. "It all fits," he agreed, wanting to kick himself for not realizing it sooner. "Katz had a motive *and* access to the special effects."

"And he was at Paula West's trailer the morning of the acid incident," Joe added. "He must have slipped the acid in the flask. Then he told us to lead the pack of zombies, putting us in range of the acid."

"I guess he rigged the chandelier over his head himself," Frank said, the pieces all slipping together in his mind. "He knew that when the lights went on, the chandelier would fall. He was taking quite a risk. The chandelier could have struck him. But it was a perfect way to convince us that he wasn't the killer. He was also the only one who knew we were heading to the Beaufort Hotel.

"And Mike said the shooting was postponed today because Katz had urgent business off the set. Everyone else on the crew stayed around today. He had to be the gunman at the theater," Frank said, shaking his head. "It was Katz all along."

"Bingo!" murmured a voice behind them. Frank whirled around to face a small closet. He lunged toward the door and threw it open, clenching his fist and drawing it back.

But then Frank froze, midpunch. A revolver protruded from the darkness of the closet, aimed at his head.

Shane Katz stepped out of the closet, grinning evilly.

Chapter 15

JOE THOUGHT about rushing Katz. The distance between them was relatively short. Maybe I can reach him, Joe thought. But he didn't like maybes, especially where his brother's safety was concerned.

"If you value your brother's life, you won't try anything funny and you'll do exactly as I say," Katz said to Joe as if he were reading his mind.

"I knew you guys would figure it out eventually," Katz said. "That's why I tried to kill you on the road and in the theater, not to mention on the set. You're both incredibly lucky. But your luck is about to change. Turn around and put your hands flat to your sides."

Frank did as Katz said, staring directly at Joe.

Frank remained calm, his expression indicating that he wanted Joe to bide his time.

Joe nodded slightly.

Katz stuck the revolver against Frank's back. "We're all going to walk over to the house. If anyone is around and you try to tip them off, I'll kill Frank without a moment's hesitation," Katz said. His voice, cold and serious, chilled Joe.

Joe stepped out of the trailer first, Frank and Katz behind him. Joe walked toward Horror House, weighing his options.

"Very good," Katz murmured from behind the Hardys.

Joe felt as if his blood were boiling. He wanted to take Katz down so badly he could taste it, but he was helpless! One ounce of pressure on the trigger, and Frank would be dead.

They were halfway to the house when Joe spotted Mike Sinnochi heading toward his trailer.

"Hi, guys," Mike said, passing them.

Joe wanted to cry out but didn't dare. Joe stared wordlessly at Mike, hoping Mike might see something was wrong. It was dark, though, and Joe knew the chances of his noticing anything were pretty slim.

Katz led them into the house and down to the basement. Katz turned on the basement light and made Joe and Frank take the steps a few feet in front of him.

As Joe stepped on the basement floor, he noticed Clervi, tied to a furnace pipe. Clervi's eyes were closed, and his head was bowed. He appeared to be unconscious. Joe rushed over to examine him, gently lifting Clervi's head. Several bruises were darkening on the actor's cheeks. One of his eyes was red and puffy.

Joe turned and fixed his gaze on Katz.

"He's alive," Katz assured Joe. "Now we're almost through with our little game. Pick a piece of rope up off the floor and tie your brother's hands."

Joe saw two short pieces of rope and reluctantly used one to tie Frank's hands behind his back.

Katz picked up the other piece of rope and told Joe to turn around. He tied Joe's hands.

"How could you brutally murder someone you've been friends with for years?" Joe demanded contemptuously.

"Friend? Friend?" Katz shouted, waving the gun around dangerously. "He wasn't my friend! He used me! Killing Warmouth was easy. That slime cheated me out of millions! When I signed the deal with Warmouth, I was inexperienced. He took advantage of me, but I got my revenge."

"I can understand the way you felt about Warmouth, but why frame Matthew?" Frank asked, the genuine curiosity in his voice a startling contrast to Joe's outrage. "What did he ever do to you?"

"He stole the limelight," Katz replied. "I'm the reason Horror House is popular. All Clervi did was read the lines from a paper, and yet the fans give him the credit I deserve. Leonard Gold maintained that a picture without Clervi would be a disaster. I think the fans would see these pictures no matter who's behind the Reaper's face. I pity Matthew, actually. You see, he was only a pawn in my little game. Pinning the murder on him was easy. So was rigging the accidents. I even sprung Clervi from that cardboard jail while the deputy was snoozing. The only thing that proved difficult was getting rid of the two of you. But I plan to rectify that matter right now."

"So you *were* the one who substituted the acid in the flask," Joe said, trying to keep Katz talking until he could figure a way to get out of his predicament.

"My dear detective," Katz said proudly, "I not only filled the flask with acid, I also substituted the real scythe for the fake one. I've been planning this for months. I shot at you on your way back from the hotel. I shot at you in the theater, because I realized you might focus your investigation on me next. I also had no desire to see Paula blamed for this murder. I've always thought highly of her."

"What about the chandelier in the dining room?" Frank inquired. "You rigged that, didn't you? You could have killed yourself."

"Yes, I suppose I could have," Katz admitted. "But no venture is without risk. I knew precisely when the chandelier would fall, and you, Joe, moved me from harm's way just before I was prepared to move myself."

"I'm beginning to wish I'd been too late," Joe muttered defiantly. "You seem awfully pleased with yourself."

Katz's laughter echoed in the basement. "That's because I am, Joe. While I pretended to mourn the death of my good friend Andrew Warmouth, the two of you were going in circles."

Katz slowly backed up the stairway, his revolver still trained on the Hardys. "You were the only things that stood in my way. I knew you would figure it out sooner or later. Now my plan is complete. I've soaked the house with gasoline. In a few minutes I'm going to set it on fire. The police will find three skeletons—yours and Clervi's—in the ashes."

Katz motioned to Clervi. "The police will receive a note that I forced Matthew to write before he passed out, taking responsibility for the deaths. He refused to write it at first, but I"—Katz paused, motioning to Clervi's bruised face—"convinced him. Poor Matthew has such a low threshold for pain. Everyone will believe that the Reaper killed both of you, too."

"Why burn the house down?" Frank asked.

"You'll mess up the end of your movie. In fact, you'll be ruining the whole series."

"Don't you get it?" Katz asked. "I don't want to do this film. I want to start all over, breathe fresh air into this series. *Horror House* has a cult following, but it could make millions more with a little more of my input. That was another thing I despised about Andy—he allowed the films to become so repetitious. As for the house, I can have a set built that will look exactly like this place."

Katz walked up to the cellar door. Before leaving, he paused and glanced down directly into Joe's eyes. "Don't take it personally, guys. That's show biz!"

Katz laughed and left the basement. The door slammed. Joe heard a lock turn.

"I can't believe I ever respected that guy," Joe muttered through clenched teeth.

Joe turned to Clervi. To his shock, Clervi's eyes were wide open. "I was acting," Clervi explained simply. "I wanted him to think I was unconscious. If you can get free, I know another way out of the basement, but we'll have to hurry."

"Frank, I bound you with loose slipknots," Joe said excitedly.

"I know," Frank said, smiling. His hands were already loose. Frank untied Joe and Clervi, who immediately led them to another stairway hidden behind the furnace. They rushed up the stairs.

Just as Joe was ready to burst through the door to freedom, Frank held him back.

"Wait," Frank cautioned his brother, reaching out and touching the door first. He quickly pulled his hand away.

"The door's burning hot!" Frank exclaimed. "We're trapped!"

Chapter 16

"WE HAVE TO TRY the main door," Joe said, taking off down the stairs. "It's our only chance to get out of here!"

Joe raced back to the stairs Katz had led them down. He tried the door at the top. It was locked. He rammed his shoulder into it, but still it wouldn't budge.

"Help me," Joe told Frank.

He and Frank both rammed their bodies against the door—and slowly they could feel it begin to give.

"Don't let up, Joe!" Frank said. "I couldn't get any leverage balancing on the stairs to kick it down, so we're going to have to keep using our shoulders!"

"No, you won't!" Clervi shouted.

Joe stared down at Clervi, who had gone back to the furnace and was now climbing the stairs with an ax in his hands.

"I found this hanging on the wall by the furnace," Clervi told them, raising the ax over his head. "Stand aside. Playing a crazed killer is finally going to pay off."

The Hardys moved, and Clervi began chopping at the door. The wood splintered, then fell away as Clervi chopped a hole big enough for Frank to slip his hand through and unlock the door. Smoke billowed into the basement from the hole.

Frank rushed out of the basement, Joe and Clervi behind him, and was met by fire on all sides of the house. Frank took off his shirt and covered his mouth with it while he tried to determine the best route. The fire was everywhere, and it looked as if they were trapped.

"This house is going up fast!" Clervi cried. "It's old and dry. We have to make it outside before the second floor collapses!"

Suddenly Sheriff Thornall appeared through a wall of fire moving at a speed that contradicted his size. Thornall had a scarf tied to his nose and mouth and was carrying a wet blanket.

"Come on," Thornall ordered, throwing the blanket over the trio. "I'm getting you out of here!"

They charged through the wall of smoke, the oppressive heat on their backs. As they raced through the kitchen, a piece of flaming ceiling fell, striking Thornall on the left shoulder and knocking him on the floor. A thick beam scraped the wall as it fell on top of the drywall covering the sheriff.

"Give me a hand, Frank!" Joe commanded, shrugging out from under the blanket.

"Get out of here, you stupid greenhorns!" Thornall shouted, trying and failing to budge the piece of ceiling.

Joe gripped one side of the beam while Frank gripped the other. It was hot. Joe could barely hold on to it. His hands felt as if they were on fire. He forced himself to hang on as he and Frank slowly began to lift the beam. Joe looked at Frank, whose expression conveyed the same pain—and the same determination.

The Hardys finally managed to roll the beam away, freeing Thornall.

Joe gripped Thornall's arm and pulled him up. "Are you okay?" he asked.

"I'm a little singed, but I'll live. Let's get out of here!" the sheriff exclaimed.

They raced through the living room, licks of flame singeing the blanket, and through the front door to safety.

After they had run several yards from the house, Joe turned back and saw that the mansion now was entirely engulfed in flame. He looked at the palms of his hands and noticed the blisters that were forming.

"Much obliged for the rescue," Thornall wheezed, bending over to catch his breath.

"Sheriff, Shane Katz is the murderer. He got away," Frank said frantically.

"Settle down. I already know. When I brought Miss West back to the set, Mike Sinnochi told me he saw Katz and you boys go into the house and that you were acting funny. I went around back and saw that the house was burning. Shane Katz ran right into me, carrying an empty gas can. He's handcuffed and waiting in the back of my car."

The whole crew was standing outside watching the house burn. Mike Sinnochi, Cathy Bowley, and Paula West rushed up to the Hardys.

"I knew you guys wouldn't walk by me without saying hi," Mike said to Joe.

"Are you sure you're okay?" Paula said, examining Clervi's bruises.

"I can't believe Shane Katz was the murderer," Cathy said, shocked.

"Believe it," Frank said. "Katz was seething with hatred toward Warmouth. He killed him to get the money he felt he had been cheated out of. He engineered the accidents and tried to kill Joe and me with firearms twice, not to mention his attempt to roast us alive."

"But why burn the house down?" Thornall wondered. "Why would Katz ruin a movie he was going to make money off of?"

"He hated the series," Joe replied. "Katz

wanted to do the films differently. Burning down the house would give him a clean slate and tons of publicity on which to base his next film."

Thornall nodded, then turned to Clervi. "Seems I had you pegged all wrong," Thornall said, extending his hand. "I hope you'll accept my apology."

"I certainly will," Clervi said, eagerly shaking Thornall's hand.

Clervi then turned to the Hardys. "No more horror movies for me," Clervi said. "I'm going to call my agent in the morning and see if that role I was offered is still open."

Joe and Frank congratulated Clervi. Firetrucks had pulled into the driveway, and fire fighters now spilled out onto the lawn, unrolling hoses to help control the blaze. Joe noticed that Harold and Kitty Hughes were also there. They walked toward him, their faces bright in the fire light. Their arms were wrapped around each other and smiles of relief were on their faces as they watched their home burn.

Kitty stepped away from Harold and hugged Clervi. "The horror is finally over," she said softly.

"Yep," Harold said to the Hardys. "The insurance money from this blaze will buy Kitty and me a new lease on life. And maybe now the spirits in the house will know peace."

Joe glanced around at everyone. They all looked happy and relieved. But he was sad because his favorite horror movie series had ended. Something else was bothering him even more, though.

"What's the matter now?" Frank asked.

"Don't you see, Frank?" Joe demanded melodramatically. "We're watching our careers as professional zombies go up in smoke!"

Frank and Joe's next case:

Long-lost treasure beckons the Hardys to a deep-sea adventure in the Bahamas when they join a crew of divers seeking to unlock the gold-laden vaults of a long-ago shipwreck. But promise soon turns to peril as the treasure hunters become the hunted—and the brothers become the targets of sabotage!

Frank and Joe discover that beneath the surface of the ocean lurk the deepest dangers. They plunge into a world of supercharged speedboat chases and underwater combat and are drawn into a deadly game in which the winners go for the gold and the losers go to the sharks . . . in *Deep Trouble,* Case #54 in The Hardy Boys Casefiles™.